P9-DZM-319

Now it was her turn to tell him what she thought

"I'm curious, Mr. Dante," she speculated haughtily. "Do you ever wonder if a woman is more interested in you or your family's money?"

He laughed. "No."

Why was he so unperturbed when her whole body screamed out her unease? Here she sat with her arms crossed over her chest and her legs twisted together so tightly she'd never be able to untangle them. Her body language, if one was a reader of such things, was declaring her the loser!

She balked at that notion. Regaining a shade of her outward composure, she demanded, "Why do you say no? Are you so conceited that you can't imagine a woman wanting you for your money?"

"Would you want me for my money?"

"No!"

He nodded, satisfied. "Thank you."

"You misunderstand, Mr. Dante. I don't want you at all!"

Dear Reader:

A writer's first book often portrays her homeland. And why not? In school we were all taught to write about what we know best. For five of Silhouette's most innovative writers, Oklahoma is more than home: Oklahoma is the blood that runs in their veins. Ada Steward, author of two Special Editions about this pioneer state, writes that Oklahoma is "a land and people still untamed beneath their veneer of civilization."

Starting with February 1986, Silhouette Special Edition is featuring the AMERICAN TRIBUTE—a tribute to America, where romance has never been so good. For six consecutive months, one out of every six Special Editions is an episode in the AMERICAN TRIBUTE, a portrait of the lives of six women, all from Oklahoma. AMERICAN TRIBUTE features some of your favorite authors—Ada Steward, Jeanne Stephens, Gena Dalton, Elaine Camp and Renee Roszel. You'll know the AMERICAN TRIBUTE by its patriotic stripe under the Silhouette Special Edition border.

AMERICAN TRIBUTE—six women, six stories.

AMERICAN TRIBUTE—one of the reasons Silhouette Special Edition is just that—special.

The Editors at Silhouette Books

★ ★ AMERICAN ★ TRIBUTE ★ ★ ★

RENEE ROSZEL
Nobody's Fool

Silhouette Special Edition

Published by Silhouette Books New York

America's Publisher of Contemporary Romance

for
Mary and Rik

SILHOUETTE BOOKS
300 East 42nd St., New York, N.Y.   10017

Copyright © 1986 by Renee Roszel

All rights reserved, including the right to reproduce
this book or portions thereof in any form whatsoever.
For information address Silhouette Books,
300 East 42nd St., New York, N.Y.   10017

ISBN: 0-373-09313-6

First Silhouette Books printing June 1986

All the characters in this book are fictitious. Any
resemblance to actual persons, living or dead, is
purely coincidental.

SILHOUETTE, SILHOUETTE SPECIAL EDITION and colophon
are registered trademarks of the publisher.

America's Publisher of Contemporary Romance

Printed in the U.S.A.

Where a man's dreams count for more than his parentage...

RENEE ROSZEL

was born and lives in Tulsa, Oklahoma, with her husband and two sons. She covers both physical as well as mental exercise by alternating her writing with teaching a class in rhythmic aerobics. She enjoys the two aspects of her work enormously and says, "It's great to be paid for things you'd do for free!"

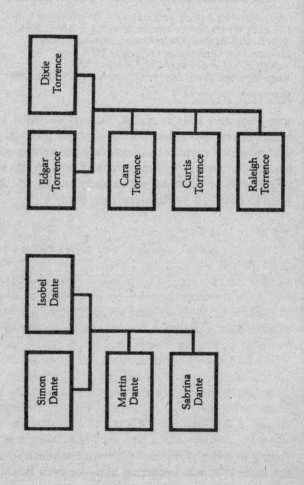

Chapter One

A pile of manure, Dante—your game was a beee-yewtiful pile of manure. Thanks." Bobby Dunlap stepped out of the shower stall, a white towel wrapped around his waist. His voice sounded muffled as he rubbed his hair with another towel. "What happened to your backhand, pal? I'd have sworn my grandma was out there on that racquetball court beatin' rugs."

Martin Dante slipped his dress shirt over his broad shoulders and narrowed his gaze. "You're just as lousy a winner as you are a loser, Dunlap. Funny it's taken me all these years to notice." He tucked the pin-striped shirt into navy slacks. Jerking the sleeves down, he fastened the cuffs brusquely. Why was he feeling so damned irritated? It wasn't so much losing the game that was bothering him—or even Bobby's nettling. It was something else, but he couldn't quite put his finger on what.

"You got somethin' tangled in your barbed wire, boy?" Bobby quizzed with a curious grin.

"Not a thing." Martin sat down on the locker room bench and began pulling on his socks. "And drop that 'good old boy' routine. Remember, I know that when you drive that pickup home it sits in a four-car garage beside a Porsche and a Caddy."

Bobby's uninhibited guffaw echoed loudly in the large, well-appointed locker room of the Tulsa Racquetball and Aerobics Club as he grabbed a pair of boots from the floor of his locker. "What's wrong, boy? Mebbe your little Miss America told you to throw yourself into your paper shredder?" he conjectured, grinning with lecherous curiosity.

"And people say you lack warmth," Martin commented dryly as he stepped into his loafers and walked to the row of porcelain sinks set into a marble countertop along a mirrored wall. Combing his straight, black hair, he gave one last short-tempered swipe at the wide silver streak at his right temple, frowning at the sober reflection. "She's not Miss America—third runner-up. And that was several years ago."

"Oh? Excuse me, she's probably old and ugly by now. You're lucky to be rid of her."

Mart checked a cut on his square, cleft chin. His mercury-blue eyes flashed with irritation at his unaccountable lack of concentration lately. How many years had it been since he'd cut himself shaving? He pursed his lips. What the hell was the matter with him lately? Even in his aggravated state, he kept his voice cool, his expression mild. "No, Bobby, Belinda and I have a date tomorrow. There's not a thing wrong, there."

"Then you're having trouble with that Mathison-Wakefield tightrope you've been walking? Is that it?"

Martin shook his head and turned back toward Bobby, a half smile crooking his lips. "Maybe it'd be better if we dropped that particular subject."

"Yeah, I know. It's gotta be a curse to be needed by both sides in an election campaign—a well-payin' curse—but still a curse. I'm just glad I'm apolitical, myself—I hate all elected officials as a matter of policy."

"I know. And it's that wild-eyed political apathy that I like about you, son," Martin admitted with a wry grin. "In an election year especially."

Bobby sat down on the bench and looked up at his friend as he tugged on one of his boots. "So you thought up the only computer software in Oklahoma that can help figure out the campaign tactics for both parties. And 'cause both sides are payin' ya, you can't bed down with either candidate." He gave out a low whistle of disbelief. "Your business reputation must be one helluva lot better than your rep with women."

Buttoning his collar around a muted paisley tie, Martin eyed his friend skeptically, "Thanks so much." He lifted his navy linen sport jacket from the hook in his locker and looked at his watch. "I've got to be out at TU to teach my computer course in thirty minutes. I'll see you same time next week."

Bobby looked up, surprised. "Say, I didn't know you were teaching a computer course."

"Continuing education for adults. It's called, 'If Computers Are So Smart, Why Can't They Speak English?''

"Amen, brother." He jabbed Martin with an elbow. "Any sexy ladies in the class?"

"I haven't noticed. Lately they're all starting to look alike." He lifted his shoulders in a slight shrug, speaking more to himself than to Bobby, "For once, I'd like to meet someone a little different—interesting."

"Interesting!" Shaking his head, Bobby chuckled. "You been cuddlin' up to machines too long!" Pulling his dark Stetson off the top of his locker, he fitted it over his sandy curls. "Well, think I'll go have a tall beer." He tapped his hat in a parting salute. "If I come up with a way to solve your problem of findin' an interestin' woman, I won't hesitate to lend a hand. S'long, buddy."

Martin slid a suspicious gaze to Bobby's back as he slid out of the door in his loose-limbed way. "Dunlap, don't do one damned thing—" The door closed and Martin's warning echoed in the empty room.

Exasperated with himself, he exhaled slowly, a feeling of doom descending like a cloud of dust. Confiding anything to Bobby was an open invitation for some sort of lunatic prank. Looking at his watch with no particular interest, Martin realized it was after six o'clock. He moved to follow Bobby, but remembered that he'd left his lecture notes in his locker. Pivoting back, he cursed his forgetfulness. Something was going to have to change in his life, and change soon.

He felt like one of his computers—sought-after and successful, yet somehow not really alive.

"Oh, darn!" Cara groaned, as she stood in the parking lot of the Racquetball and Aerobics Club. "Will you pleeeaaase open your mouth, you rotten car? I don't have time for this!" She thumped a fist on the hood of her middle-aged economy car. With a vigor born of frustration and a rapidly approaching deadline, she tugged on the stuck hood. "Come on, you piece of junk!"

"May I help?" Martin doubted the wisdom of delaying his start to the University of Tulsa, but his deeply entrenched chivalry won out over his need to get to his class on time.

Cara looked up, startled by his quiet approach. "You and..." She faltered to a halt when she recognized the man standing next to her. But reminding herself that he was merely a man, like any other, nothing more, she squared her shoulders and finished, "...a wrecking ball." Stepping away from the grillwork, which was making a waffle pattern on her bare legs, she flung an exasperated hand toward the car. "This rattletrap has failed me again, and I have to be at TU at six-thirty to teach a class." She paused to breathe a tired sigh, dropping her eyes to her scanty attire. "And I still have to change."

Martin scanned her slender form and smiled appreciatively. "You're the aerobics teacher here, aren't you?" He extended a hand. "I'm Martin Dante."

She accepted his hand briefly, noticing with some interest that he revealed his identity without the snobbish air of superiority she would have expected. "I know who you are, Mr. Dante."

"Really?" He lifted a brow in apparent surprise. "What do you teach at TU that you have to change for?"

"At night I teach a self-discovery course through the Continuing Education department." A gust of summer wind pressed past them, and she swept a strand of curly hair out of her eyes. "By day, I'm an adjunct professor in sociology."

He grinned. "College professors have changed since I went to school."

For a spoiled brat, Mr. Dante had an easy—but false—charm. Of course she already knew that. It was a huge part of the man's problem. But his problems weren't her problems. Right now she had a class to teach. She forced her question through thinned lips. "Look, would you mind if I ride to the campus with you?"

His expression registered vague surprise. "Not at all. I was about to suggest it." Lightly touching her elbow, he directed her toward his sporty Mercedes. "Tell me, Miss..." He paused to allow her to fill in the blanks.

"Torrence." She reached back and carelessly lifted the heavy mane of hair off her shoulders. It was hot for June.

His nod was thoughtful, and she wondered if he was surprised that she hadn't offered her first name. She couldn't tell from his complacent expression.

"Miss Torrence?" he asked. "How did you know I was going to the university?"

A scornful smile lifted her lips. He must be kidding! "Mr. Dante, I've lived in Tulsa all my life, and for as long as I can remember, everything you've said and done has been recorded in the society section of our newspaper. I've read about you for years."

He gazed at her, his expression registering curiosity. "You don't look like the type who would follow such things."

She blanched and turned away, fighting the urge to ask him what, in his opinion, she had too little of to be 'the type'—money or class? With a regal lift of her chin, she worked for nonchalance in her tone. "Thank you." Her voice sounded strained, even so. She could feel his eyes on her, but she refused to meet his glance. Instead, she forged on as though she hadn't a care in the world. "As a sociologist, I'm interested in all types of collective behavior. Tulsa's privileged class has a mode of accepted behavior all its own—interesting to observe."

He unlocked the passenger door and held it for her. "Had I known I was being clinically observed by such an attractive researcher all these years, I'd have spent more time polishing my modes."

"Or having your butler polish them," she mumbled under her breath as she slid into the leather bucket seat.

He closed the door and circled the car. Her smile was twisted and melancholy. Here she was, speaking to Martin Dante again after seventeen years. He, of course, would have no reason to remember her. To him, she had just been a mud-streaked, seventeen-year-old girl with a mop in her hands.

She remembered him vividly, though. Martin was a local celebrity of the wealthy set even at twenty. He had stopped by her family's small grocery story late one night, several hours after their hot-water heater had burst, wreaking havoc. Back then, they'd lived in a small apartment above her parents' shop in downtown Tulsa—long ago torn down in urban renewal. That night, she, her brother and sister and her parents had scrambled out of bed into old clothes and had literally plunged into the watery mess below.

Drudgery-filled hours later, with most of the water damage repaired, Dixie, Cara's mother, had shooed the other siblings upstairs, leaving just Cara and her dad to do the final mopping-up. It had been shortly after midnight when she had heard the knock on the door.

She recalled how her body had gone rigid; all hot at first, and then cold. Her mouth gaped at the beautiful Martin Dante, dressed impeccably in a tuxedo, standing there like Prince Charming, smiling at her. She had been able to do no more than stare, in some sort of teenage daze, as her father let the young man in. It had been the sound of high-pitched giggling that brought her around, and she'd winced to see an attractive blonde swathed in pink chiffon float through the door and attach a pale hand to his.

He'd explained to her father that he and his date had just come from the Cinderella Ball, and needed to use the phone. The Cinderella Ball was a gala event in Tulsa that only the privileged attended. Most youngsters, like Cara, could only dream about such parties.

Cara had cast her eyes away, but her ears remained alert against her will.

Much to her distress, the blonde giggled again, gushing that Martin's Corvette's tires had been removed while they'd been at the dance. Cara couldn't help turning back. Unable to stop herself, she gasped. "Somebody stole your tires?"

The blonde covered her mouth and laughed, leaning heavily against Martin. "Not really. It was a practical joke! There was a note on the windshield." She swayed a little, and Cara realized she had been drinking. "Sooooooo—" the girl threw out a hand "—here I am, like Cinderella. My coach has turned into a pumpkin and I have no way to get home from the ball!" The last word was little more than a squeak as she burst into a renewed fit of giggles.

"Princess Grace, maybe, but not Cinderella." Martin had grinned then, that beautifully crooked, often photographed grin, and had shaken his head. "You've never been near the business end of a broom." As his date giggled, Cara's father led Martin toward the small office in the rear of the store where the phone was.

Cara followed Martin's movements covertly beneath her lashes, admiring the breadth of his shoulders, and the way the black velvet fit across them. They swayed just enough as he walked to make his gait graceful—in a completely masculine way. She sighed deeply. Unconsciously she'd rested her chin on her hands, folded loosely over the tip of the mop handle. When the blonde spoke again, her closeness startled Cara, and she jumped, poking herself with the mop.

"Ouch!" she groaned, rubbing the bruise under her chin. The mop handle clattered to the floor, and the girl had to jump to get out of its way.

"Watch it! My dress," she snapped, gathering the chiffon about her legs.

"I—I'm sorry," Cara stammered, turning to face her.

She shrugged then, still examining the fragile gown. "There's no harm done, I guess." She met Cara's gaze and gasped. "My God! What's all over your face? Mud?"

Cara rubbed her cheek, confused. "I—I don't know."

"On second thought, I'd rather not know." She giggled again. "You really get into your work. Mom might be able to use you sometime—after one of my pool parties. Things tend to get out of hand, sometimes. What's the name of the cleaning service you work for?"

"Uh—I don't—that is—I live here. We had a...a problem with the hot water heater."

"Oh." She waved off her mistake. "Well still, if you'd like to make a little extra money..." Martin and Mr. Torrence came out of the office, and she let the sentence drop, apparently losing interest in the subject.

Cara, likewise, dismissed the girl from her thoughts, her heartbeat increasing with each step Martin took toward them. When he reached the blond girl's side, he slid a casual arm about her shoulders. "Dad said he'd meet us at his office. He's calling security there so they'll know to let us in." He turned to face Cara.

"Your father told me about the hot-water heater. Sorry about the mess."

Cara managed to whisper, "It's not your fault."

The blonde burst out in a loud fit of giggles. "I have it, Martin! Here's your Cinderella!" She reached out and took Cara's chin between her fingers. "Just look at that face! Isn't it a sight?"

Cara had felt humiliated at being discussed by this thoughtless young woman as though she weren't there. Even after all these years she could remember how her cheeks had burned, and the feeling of fingernails scraping her skin when she'd jerked her face away. Tremendous family pride squared her shoulders, and she had met Martin's gaze straight on. The silver-blue orbs had been narrowed slightly and he was nodding. Cara recalled her shock at noticing he was actually agreeing with his date's cruel remark.

His chuckle was soft, but it cut like the sharpest blade as he'd murmured, "Yes, quite a sight—now that I see that face up close." He'd winked at Cara, then, and she'd turned to ashes inside. How dare he be so conceited, so superior, to think that all it took from him was a smile and a wink to be forgiven for making fun of someone! Did he think money exempted him from common decency?

He was a despicable, spoiled brat. She'd opened her mouth to tell him so, but realized he'd dropped his gaze and had a hand in his breast pocket. As she reached out to get his attention, or hit him—she hadn't been quite sure which she would have actually done— he laid a ten dollar bill in her outstretched hand. "Here, Cinderella—for the inconvenience."

With the bill thrust at her, his warm hand on hers, she was momentarily struck dumb. In mortified silence she watched as he turned toward his date. "And as for you—I think coffee is in order." He led her away out the door, and in his wake went any starry-eyed ideas about Martin Dante. The ugly truth was, behind that gorgeous face was the supreme insensitive snob. And for seventeen years she'd considered herself lucky not to have run into him again—not until today.

Her family hadn't been poor. They hadn't had much money, but they were never hungry, and never in doubt about being loved and supported in anything they chose to do. And Cara had chosen early on to become a professional—subservient to no one. She worked very hard to make it through college and get her Master's degree in sociology. She was pleased with her accomplishments, and her family was proud of her. She loved the mental exercise her professorial duties demanded, as well as her rigorous aerobics classes at the club. Her life was good and full—if singular, at times.

Some people might say Cara had gone too far—become a wild-eyed radical in fact—about not being anyone's servant. She pulled her lips together realizing that most of those "people" were men.

The irony was that it was men who had made her that way. Her convictions about men and marriage had been forged in the fires of two engagements. It had devastated her when her first fiancé broke their engagement just two days before the wedding. Heartbroken, she'd decided it had been all her fault. If she'd been more giving, more attentive, he wouldn't have left. Then, two years later, when she'd become engaged again, she'd bent over backward to be everything her fiancé had wanted in a woman.

She'd tried to learn to cook, hating every minute of it. She'd sent in her resignation when he'd said he didn't want her to work. She'd compromised and given in to his demands, doing everything in her power to make the man happy. She'd fawned and backslapped when his ego needed strokes, getting nothing in return except to be taken for granted. But in the final analysis, he'd dumped her for the daughter of his boss.

She'd played all the "love me-serve me" games, and she'd learned the hard way. Never again would she compromise herself for a man. For the past three years, she'd bruised a lot of male egos, and had been called everything from a "fire-breathing witch" to a "coldhearted iron maiden." She told herself she didn't care. It was better than being a servant who got paid for her services with a broken heart!

She'd erected her spiky barriers with such single-mindedness that she was able to look upon the male sex with cool disdain. At least she'd thought she could. She stared down at her hands, fisted in her lap. Apparently, Martin Dante was one man who could still raise her ire. It was funny how that girlhood humiliation still hurt so after all these years. Even the memory of her two broken engagements didn't sting like the echo of Martin Dante's glib rudeness.

It made her uncomfortable to realize a man could still have any power over her emotions—even if the

emotion elicited was hate. She preferred indifference.
That way she could always keep the upper hand. The
driver's door clicked open, and she took a deep
breath, anxious for this ride to be over and almost
panicked because comfortable indifference had not
settled over her like a coat of armor. Pretending a
nonchalance she didn't feel, she turned toward him in
time to see a muscular thigh mold to light-blue slacks
as he slid into the driver's seat. Gritting her teeth she
shifted to stare out of the windshield.

He settled on the red leather and turned the key. The
car rumbled with the guttural authority that many
thousands of dollars could muster. Inclining his dark
head toward her, he said, "My parents have a butler,
Miss Torrence—and a cook. I live alone in a two-
bedroom condominium. And though I've never actually polished modes, I do polish my shoes—also
alone." He paused. "Now that that's cleared up, is it
Miss, Mrs. or Ms. Torrence?"

She'd forgotten her mumbled gibe, and his quiet
rejoinder caught her off guard. Hoping that he
couldn't tell how uneasy she was, she crossed her legs
to exhibit in body language that she was totally unbothered by his quiet reprimand.

"Call me Professor Torrence. I worked hard for the
title, and I love to hear people say it." Why give him
anything?

He was still smiling, but his dark brows dipped
slightly together over his straight, aristocratic nose.
" 'Professor' it is, then." He turned to look through the
windshield as they glided out of the club's parking lot.

"I teach the computer course—"

"I know," she interrupted. "Ben Bandy taught it before his company transferred him. Ben was an excellent teacher." She emphasized the word "Ben," with no remorse.

He braked the car at a stoplight and turned half-lowered lids in her direction. "As opposed to me?"

"I really couldn't say, Mr. Dante." She lifted a hand to the nape of her neck, again moving her hair away. His air-conditioning was marvelous. Hers, as usual, had quit functioning with the first gust of hot wind. Waving a hand in casual dismissal, she drew battle lines and blasted him with cannon fire from behind her battlements. "All I've heard is that enrollment for that class has doubled—mainly female. It's still up in the air whether it's your computer know-how or your money that interests them."

His deep chuckle reverberated throughout the small car. "Are you always this direct, professor?"

"Of course." That was a lie, but she felt no compunction about it. "I think we'd all be better off if everyone told the absolute truth."

He maneuvered the car smoothly through the last crush of rush-hour traffic, and Cara absently scanned the businesses along Harvard Avenue as they whizzed by.

After a moment of concentrated silence, he offered, "Interesting theory—this absolute truth thing." When he didn't go on, she turned to look at his profile. Evidently he had been waiting for her to do that, for as soon as her attention was drawn to him, he asked, "Don't you think that it can hurt sometimes?"

"Yes, it can." She set her jaw. "I'd love to know at what tender age you discovered that fact."

He turned toward her. "What do you mean?"

She recrossed her legs and turned away. "Never mind." After a moment, she couldn't stand the silence, so she added, "Mind you, I'm not advocating it for everyone. I just happen to feel that it's right for me." She nodded her head with firm decision. "I prefer the direct approach to people. Be...honest and up front. That way you always know where you stand."

"Hmm." He absorbed her thoughts quietly for a moment, and Cara watched with some concern. His eyes caught her attention. The crazy notion flashed across her mind that here was a man who really had what her mother had always referred to as bedroom eyes. Before she could squelch the ridiculous mental exercise, she found herself wondering just how many bedrooms those eyes had seen.

Belatedly she managed to crush the thought as the subtle crease of a dimple appeared in his cheek. He was smiling. With a flash of high irritation, she had an overwhelming urge to wipe that grin off his arrogant face.

"Do you dare test my theory, Mr. Dante?" She lifted her chin, a challenging smile lifting her lips. He wouldn't have the guts.

He maneuvered the car onto Eleventh Street. "Sounds dangerous."

"I dare you."

"To what?"

His quick, speculative glance toward her seemed vaguely disturbed. Good! She had him worried. Why not scratch away at some of that platinum polish? "To speak the truth—the complete truth—and be able to take it, too, during the rest of this ride. I'm sure in your younger years you must have told some woman the absolute truth, at least once, no matter how it hurt her."

"Never, professor."

"Never say 'never,'" she suggested a little thinly. "Anyway, what could it hurt for you to tell me what you think of me? Come on. I dare you."

"I haven't taken a dare in a lot of years." He braked at a stoplight and turned toward her. There was a strange glint in his eyes. "But I must admit, you tempt me." His smile was as striking as it was challenging. "But you'll have to start since you're the expert."

For some reason, she suddenly felt tentative about going ahead with this. That look made her uneasy. With a spasmodic swallow, she tried, "On second thought, it wouldn't be fair to you to force you into something you're so unaccustomed—"

"Your age would be a good place to start. Women usually lie about that. Most women, rather." He turned back to watch the traffic. "But a devotee of total truth such as you would never stoop to such tactics." Apparently unconcerned about being at a disadvantage, he took charge. "If you don't mind I'll start. When I first saw you, Professor, I said to myself, 'Dante, that woman doesn't look a day over forty.' Are you over forty?"

She corrected. "Thirty-four."

"Oh? Some women would have been offended by my mistake. Lucky I said it to a woman who thrives on complete honesty."

She flushed, but maintained a proud facade. "Lucky..." He continued to look straight ahead, but she could see a slight twitch at the corners of his mouth. He enjoyed that little shot.

With a shift of the gears, he asked easily, "Now, how old do you think I am?"

She slid narrowed eyes over the wood grain of his dash. "You're thirty-seven. Remember the surprise costume party some of your cronies threw for you at the Petroleum Club last month?"

He nodded. "Oh. I forgot. You read about me. That does put me at a disadvantage. But I'm game if you are. What do you say we go on?"

She spread her hands on her thighs to keep from clenching them into fists. Whatever he decided to dish out, she could take—or her name wasn't Cara Torrence! "Sure." She tried to sound thrilled. "This is going to be fun."

"You may be right." His lips quivered, and she could tell that he was smothering a smile. "My turn."

He slanted a casual glance at Cara. "This won't take long." His light eyes glittered with unrestrained humor, and Cara felt a distressing need to cover her ears with her hands. "Your hair looks like you curled it with a waffle iron."

She pulled her cheeks between her teeth and bit down. Her light-brown hair was permed in a rather curly lionesque, but perfectly acceptable, style. It was easy to take care of, suiting her active life. She swallowed hard as he unleashed volley two. "Why any otherwise attractive—albeit flat-chested—woman would do that to herself is beyond me."

Holding her breath, she forgot that she was trying not to ball her fists, while she fought a sickening urge to cross her arms in front of her small—albeit insulted—chest. How dare he! He had no business getting that personal!

"Aaaahhh..." She exhaled, faking an unbothered facade. "Wasn't that refreshing? I mean, a man like you probably had only the rarest opportunity to tell a woman the absolute truth. It must be hell for you 'gentlemen' to feel as though you must be polite and complimentary to everything that comes down the pike, just because it's wearing a skirt."

He pursed his lips. "Or a bra? I noticed you aren't wearing one. Of course I'm not complaining."

A shiver of embarrassment made her teeth rattle, and she clamped them together as she cast a furtive glance down at herself. This time, she lost the fight not to cross her arms before her leotard top.

Martin's cough—or more correctly, she was sure, his fight to keep from laughing—told her that he hadn't missed her protective move, and Cara felt her face go purple. Irritation stiffened her spine. It was her turn, damn him! Twisting around to face him more directly, she speculated haughtily. "I'm curious, Mr. Dante, do you ever wonder if a woman is more interested in you or your family's money?"

He reared back and laughed. "No."

Why was he so unperturbed when her whole body screamed out her unease? Here she sat with her arms crossed like cinched rope around her chest. Her legs were bound together so tightly that she'd never be able to untangle them. If one was a reader of body language, the twisted wreckage of her body was declaring her the loser!

She balked at that notion. Cara Torrence was not a loser! Regaining a shade of her outward composure, she charged. "Why do you say no? Are you so conceited that you can't imagine a woman wanting you for your money?"

"Would you want me for my money?"

"No!" she expelled in a shocked whisper.

He nodded, satisfied. "Thank you."

She frowned. "You misunderstand, Mr. Dante, I don't want you at all!"

The car came to a stop, and Cara blinked, swiveling her head to look out of the windshield. They were in the parking lot behind the Continuing Education building. Martin cleared his throat. "Six-twenty. If we hurry, we both can make our classes on time." How odd that this degrading episode hadn't seemed much longer! Martin looked over at her, his smile completely genuine, almost boyish. He didn't appear to be disturbed by anything she had said. On the contrary. He seemed to be in a better mood now than earlier at the aerobics club. How unfair! He'd made her miserable!

He was asking, "Where shall we meet after class?"

"Meet?" Squinting skeptically, she pushed back the heavy mass of hair—her waffled hair! "What for?"

"You need a ride home, don't you?"

"I'll take a taxi."

He swung his big body around, resting an arm casually on the teak steering wheel. "Mind if I'm perfectly frank?"

She clenched her teeth so tightly that she thought she could hear them crumbling. The man had no mercy!

When she didn't respond, he went on, "Isn't it true that any money you make tonight would have to go for cab fare? You need the money you make, Professor. Don't squander it because of foolish pride."

She tipped her pert nose an inch more directly toward the sky. "Money is not the point, Mr. Dante. I just don't care to spend any more time with you than I already have. And surely you'd prefer not to be seen with…a sight like me. I wouldn't consider putting you through that."

His crooked smile became skeptical. "Say, I haven't hurt your feelings, have I?" Leveling those sleepy eyes on her, he sobered immediately. "Good Lord. Have I?"

Distressed to hear the pity in his voice, she uttered a flat denial. "Don't be ridiculous." She turned toward the door, muttering begrudgingly, "Thanks for the ride." His hand on her shoulder halted her.

"I apologize, Professor. I'm really sorry. To prove it, I insist you let me drive you home." He reached across her and unlatched her door. "I'll meet you in the university coffee shop at eight-thirty."

The door swung open at his push. Still very disinclined to accept a ride with him, her mind stumbled around, reaching for a plausible excuse. Who else did she know that might give her a ride home? Surely there was somebody here at night that she had become acquainted with, who would be leaving around then. She slid her legs out of the car for a quick exit, calling back, "No, I couldn't."

"Professor?" He squeezed her shoulder, holding her in light captivity as he asked, "What if I said you have the nicest legs I've ever seen on a college teacher? Then would you let me give you a lift home?"

One corner of her lips lifted, but there was no humor in the smile. Her hazel eyes shot sparks as she challenged. "And just how many college teachers' legs have you seen?"

"If there are many like yours, not nearly enough."

She felt an odd melting, and steeled herself against it. She shouldn't accept the ride home. Still, she hadn't really had her chance at him yet. Somehow, it had become important that she embarrass him—humiliate him—just once. She might be able to use tonight's class project to make him as uncomfortable as he had made her. With an overstated dip of her shoulder, she pulled out from under his hand and slid out of the car, calling back, "If you insist. Eight-thirty."

Chapter Two

Cara tripped on the steps in front of the Student Union building and grabbed the railing between her forearms and her breastbone. Her eyes became hazel saucers that contrasted starkly with the white background of grease paint that masked her face. "Darn these shoes," she grumbled, wondering how men who wore size tens ever walked up steps! Grimacing, she shook her head. Maybe it wasn't such a good idea after all.

"You okay?" a timid voice asked at her back.

Remembering that she was supposed to be a clown, she ignored her discomfort and turned to face the inquirer. With a sweeping, disjointed bow, she mimed her thanks for the young man's concern, before thrusting a gloved hand to her chest to indicate that she was hale and hearty. She dropped a bowlegged curtsy to the female student who was standing beside the youth. Then, she bounded up the rest of the steps two at a time until she reached the top. Cara flung herself around and dropped in a gape-kneed squat, her arms dangling, her elbows high and her head lolling to the side. To the staring students, she looked like a large puppet hanging from invisible string.

Her hair was tied up with multicolored twine in ten pigtails tipped in a garish purple fluorescent paint. She wore a large white T-shirt, over which was tied a brightly flowered bikini top. Long black tights hid her legs, and a calf-length straw hula skirt undulated in the late-evening breeze. Jogging shoes nearly twice too long for her feet, one blue and one white, were topped by two different kinds of argyle socks. A plastic lei of purple petals flopped about her neck. As she turned away, she indicated, by exaggeratedly pointing, for them to read the sign pinned to her back. It read "Ms. How-a-ya?" When she turned back, she lifted her shoulders and her hands encased in flowered garden-gloves as if to ask the same question in mime.

The two students laughed.

Cara threw them a kiss before she swivel-hipped around and walked away. One gloved palm rested on her hip. The other arm was thrust before her like a fishing pole, her hand flipped forward, wrist high, as though ready to receive a kiss from the next admirer. She pulled open the heavy door and headed toward the coffee shop in long, Groucho Marx stride, the loose sole of one shoe announcing her approach with its schlepping echo down the near empty hall.

For some odd reason, her heart began a mysterious thundering. Why was she nervous? She'd done her clown routine with her self-discovery classes lots of times—out in public. So why did this impending encounter with Martin Dante make her feel uneasy? Certainly she wasn't interested in his approval! The whole point of her staying in costume tonight was to jolt him.

The door of the coffee shop loomed before her. Already several heads had lifted and the surprised spectators were staring and poking their companions. She struck an outlandish pose. One big foot rested waist high on the door jamb, and the opposite hand shaded her eyes as though she were a sea captain searching the horizon for a speck of land. Instead of land, she was scanning the heads for one particular black and silver one.

With that hair and those broad shoulders, he wasn't hard to find. He was sitting alone at a table in the far corner. His back was to her and he appeared to be engrossed in whatever he was reading. She breathed a sigh of relief that he hadn't seen her yet. Surprise was always an asset when shock was the objective. As she watched, he picked up a cup of coffee and sipped. It was obvious that he was not waiting for her with the breathless excitement of a child waiting for Santa Claus. With a determined, if sloppy gallop, she hurried to his table and flung a leg over the chair next to his.

He turned at the sound of her foot clunking into the back of the fiberglass. His light eyes settled on the mammoth relic, and held there. Taking advantage of his surprised pause, she nodded the scuffed sneaker up and down so that the sole flapped at him.

He cleared his throat, and set his coffee mug on the table. Those lazy eyelids remained at half-mast as he lifted his gaze to her face. When she was sure his eyes were on her white mask, she pulled a melancholy pout. Her painted expression was that of a sad clown, complete with a blue teardrop on one cheek. Because her class in self-discovery dictated that they discover interesting facets of their personality by acting out their chosen clown character, without words, she decided not to talk here, either. Cocking a painted brow, she waited.

Martin shifted in his chair so that he could face her more directly. Laying his technical magazine on the table, he crossed his arms before him. "The 'Make Me Over' seminar is tomorrow night, madam. I suggest strongly that you attend."

She opened her mouth for a pantomimed "ha-ha-ha," bobbing her head, and soundlessly pounded her raised knee. But for the exaggerated roll of her eyeballs, one would have thought she really enjoyed his remark. If the truth were known, she had found his wit to be quicker than she had anticipated. That was a fact, she promised herself, that Mr. Dante would never become acquainted with.

Lifting her foot off the chair, she turned her back and pointed with both hands to her sign.

"Ms. How-a-ya," he repeated, shaking his head. "Alias Professor Torrence, if I may hazard a guess."

She turned around and plopped in the chair. With her elbows on the table, she dug her chin into her palms and nodded. Her lips lifted at the corners. The sad face, when contorted in a smile, made her appear near tears.

Martin cast a narrow glance about them. "I know how you feel. I'm not too crazy about you being Professor Torrence, either. Do you realize this room got as still as death when you slung that ridiculous clodhopper over the chair?"

Cara feigned surprise, and put an oversize glove to her ear, pretending to listen with a pained expression of concentration.

He leaned toward her. "What the hell did you say you teach, anyway, rodeo clowning?"

She curled her upper lip at him and bounded to her feet. That did it. Now it was his turn! Her mind scrambled for some appropriate humiliation. What was important to him?

His hair! She had never seen it when it was even slightly mussed, even in photos of him racing in the Tulsa Run! He must have a real thing about keeping it perfect. With an impish glint in her eye, she ran her hand heavily forward through his hair. The suede palm of the glove did an exemplary job of standing it on its ends. With one finger, she ruffed the silver streak, before poking her finger in his ear. She patted her eccentric coiffure with a flirtatious wink, as if to say, 'Come up and see me some time, big boy.'

He sat back, his brows dipping suspiciously at her behavior. "Perhaps I should have said, 'Rodeo clowning—bring your own bull,'" he amended. There was a vague but definite tenseness in his voice now.

Cara couldn't suppress a smile. Eureka! Finally, she was getting to him!

After disengaging her finger from his ear, he brushed his hand through his hair to repair the damage. Enough of his hair. She reached for his tie, but before she could get it undone, he grasped her hands. "That's enough, Harpo," he growled under his breath. Rising quickly to his feet, he released one of her hands and headed toward the exit with broad, purposeful strides.

Cara made her exit as true to the clowning tradition as she could, under the circumstances. She swung her hips and threw kisses to the small group of laughing students and faculty, lifting the hand that held her by the wrist as though she had won this handsome male trophy, and he couldn't wait to be alone with her.

But as she flounced out of the door, she began to wonder what was going to happen to her once she was alone with Mr. Martin Dante. She hadn't thought about the consequences of mussing his hair and pretending to undress him. It had been a spontaneous attempt to get a rise out of him. She had certainly done that. His expression had been a rather dashing combination of discomfort and annoyance when he had taken her hands from his tie. She doubted that he had ever been closer than a ten-foot stack of hundred-dollar bills to such a humbling experience before. And she also doubted that she still had a ride home.

He pushed through the double doors that took them out into the starry darkness, and pulled her down the steps. When they reached the sidewalk that led back to the parking lot, he turned toward her. His jaw worked angrily as he growled, "I hope nobody in there recognized you."

Cara's comically drawn brows twisted in confusion. She hadn't expected him to comment on who might have known her! Forgetting her playacting, she stuttered, "What? Why would that matter?"

He shook his head. "I would think that a professor of sociology would not care to look like a painted trollop displaying her wares in a public place—even in fun. That sort of suggestiveness, even under the guise of clowning, diminishes you as a serious scholar in some people's eyes."

Cara stared, disbelieving. "Are you serious? You can't think that anyone in that room actually believed that I was...pretending to solicit you?"

"Of course that's what they thought you were doing. For God's sake, that *is* what you were doing!"

"No, I wasn't. I was just trying to—to get a rise out of you."

"Congratulations. But the question on everyone's mind was 'what kind of a rise?'" He turned toward the parking lot, still pulling her in his firm grasp.

"Not that kind!" she defended hotly. "Let go of my arm. I've got to call a taxi."

He halted abruptly and pivoted to face her, and Cara's sticky white face collided with his navy sport coat.

"Oh, no," she groaned miserably, knowing what the white grease had done to his coat. She'd just ruined a jacket that couldn't have cost less than a week's salary—hers, not his.

He let go of her wrist and took her by the shoulders, putting distance between them; just enough distance so that she could stare forlornly at a ghostlike impression of her forehead and nose on his lapel. She closed her eyes, sighing again. "Lord..."

He released her shoulders. "It's a little late to call for outside help."

She opened her eyes to scan his stern expression. Resigned to her fate, she offered quietly, "I'll get you a new jacket. What's your size, and where did you get it?"

He shook his head. "I order my clothes from New York. Were you planning a trip there in the near future?"

She gritted her teeth as she imagined how she was going to live for the next month—without money. The picture was bleak. If he ordered his clothes from New York—probably from some designer—she might just as well multiply her original guess at the cost of the sports jacket by about four. When she spoke again, her intentions were excellent, but her voice was a little weak. "I...I'll...could I pay you back in installments?"

He snorted derisively. "Forget it, professor." Taking her by the elbow, he led her toward the car. "Let's go."

His amused dismissal stung her pride. He obviously didn't think there was any way she could pay for his damned, expensive clothes! Stiffening, she blurted, "No! I insist on paying for the coat. It was my fault."

"It was my fault. I yanked you into me," he muttered. "Let's just forget about it and try to have an accident-free ride home."

She yanked against his hold, pulling free. "No. I couldn't. I insist on taking a taxi, and I insist on paying for that coat."

He took her arm again as though he'd accidentally let his hand slip away. Ignoring her protest, he changed the subject. "Next time you want to do your clown act, just stay away from street-lamp humor. Okay?"

She peered at him, trying not to look at the white smudge on the dark coat. It was fine with her if they didn't talk about the coat. It probably was just as much his fault as hers. And she might as well forget about a taxi and go along with him. He wasn't giving her much choice in the matter. With a heavy sigh, deciding to humor him, she asked, "What would you have preferred I'd done?"

He pursed his lips in apparent thought. "You could have poured my coffee over my head."

"But that would have ruined your..." She let the sentence drop. Her face grew so fiery that she was sure that the grease on her face was hot enough to fry eggs.

It surprised her to hear an easy chuckle rumble in his chest. "What are a few minutes either way to a doomed sport coat?"

He held her elbow more tightly as he helped her off the curb onto the parking lot pavement. As they neared his car, he asked, "Just what do you think a person can discover about himself dressed up in a clown suit?"

She shrugged, and her plastic lei fell off one shoulder. Lifting it back, she answered, "It frees you up, let's you do things you wouldn't do otherwise."

"Did you learn that from a bank robber?"

She slanted him a dark look. "You think you're being sarcastic, but you're right. It does allow a certain anonymity. That's the whole point. But it's more than just getting away with things." She stepped back while he opened the passenger door for her. Slipping inside, she was careful to gather up her straw skirt between her legs so that it wouldn't be sheered away by the door.

When he got in behind the wheel, he coaxed. "Okay. It's more than anonymity for flirting in coffee shops and robbing banks."

She crossed one leg over the pile of straw she wore on her other leg. The big shoe rubbed against his pant leg. Quickly, she uncrossed her legs. Not only did she not want to initiate any physical contact with him, she also dreaded the idea of ruining his pants. "Uh—well, take me for instance. I'm supposed to be a sad clown named Ms. How-a-ya. Right?"

He ignited the engine and looked in the rearview mirror as he backed out of his parking spot. He didn't speak, but his nod told her that he was with her so far.

"I was brought up to always smile and be pleasant. Dad and Mom ran a grocery—" She stopped abruptly, clearing her throat. She didn't want to go into that with him! "Well, that's not important. What is, is that sometimes I just don't feel like being pleasant and smiling all the time—"

His caustic laugh interrupted her. With a lazy look he suggested, "I think you've overcome those urges to be pleasant."

"When I want your opinion, Mr. Dante, I'll beg you for it." She crossed her arms with an air of dismissal, before she continued. "Anyway, sometimes I feel as though the pleasant faces I see around me are nothing but plastic masks—much more phony than anything my students have ever done in my clowning exercise. You might be surprised how therapeutic such an experience can be."

"I'd be very surprised."

Lifting skeptical eyes to meet his profile, she was surprised to see him looking down at her, his lips open in an undisguised grin. Her expression closed suspiciously. "Why are you grinning at me like that?"

His eyes flitted over her, glistening like silver in the darkness. "I guess it's that hair—all those colors."

"No improvement over the waffle look, huh?" She eyed his grinning face grimly. "Have you ever considered that you might have impossibly high standards when it comes to sociology professors?"

"Why impossibly?" he queried, braking at a light.

"You probably insist that they like you," she returned pertly, turning away from him.

His laugh reverberated in the small car. "The light's green. Right or left?"

She crossed her left leg over her right and kept her eyes on the darkened sky. "Right. If you're really serious about taking me home, I live at the Landmark condominiums. They're at Ninety-first and Yale—"

"I know where they are." He pulled out into the traffic, still chuckling. "Do you want to hear a coincidence?"

A shudder of apprehension snaked up her spine. Surely he wasn't going to say he lived there, too. A man like Martin Dante couldn't sneak into a place to live without anyone knowing. Besides, all the condos had been sold. She inhaled slowly. "I'm not sure."

"Do you know Rosie and Maury Huerter?"

She relaxed. Yes, she did. They lived in the condominium below hers. "Sure. They're a nice couple. But they left last week for six months. Maury's in the oil business and they're spending some time in Brazil on a project."

"I know. I'm leasing their place from them while my house is being built in Hunter's Pointe just around the bend."

She stiffened to the purple ends of her hair. "You're...?" She licked her painted lips and grimaced at the bitter taste. Jerking to look directly at him, she began to figure wildly how she might be able to move out before he moved in! If only she could say that she was going to Brazil for six months—or maybe six years in the Antarctic! That would be even better. But rarely did the University of Tulsa send professors away like that—at least it had never happened so far in the school's history. She tried to be conversational, not wanting him to know how horrible the news was for her. "When are you moving in?"

"Last weekend. Wasn't much to it, since they left their furniture. I just had mine stored."

"Oh. I spent most of that weekend at an aerobics clinic." She so wanted to add "where they told me I was being transferred to Antarctica for six years." No such luck.

Why did she feel such panic? After all, he was only a man—only a wealthy, virile, extremely well-known figure, a man who thought she was built like a little boy, who thought she was a bizarre freak with ugly hair and no class. A man who could make her fly into a rage with the crook of his finger—or the wink of an eye.

Why had she worked and saved so long and hard to be able to put the down payment on the lovely, two-bedroom home of her dreams in a nice neighborhood? Why wouldn't she want Martin Dante for a neighbor? Why wouldn't she want smallpox?

She cleared her throat. "Hunter's Pointe is a lovely development—secluded in all those huge oaks and cedars. How long do you think construction will take?"

"I hope to be in about Thanksgiving."

Cara mentally tallied the months. Tomorrow would be July the first—nearly five. She pursed her lips. "I hope you're in earlier than that."

"That's nice of you. But I doubt it."

Pressing the edge of her thumbnail between her lips, she fought the need to tell him that niceness had nothing to do with it. This was not a man she wanted underneath—beneath—*a floor below her!*

"Don't bite your nails, Professor."

She jumped. He had actually driven her to that! She thought she'd gotten over chewing her nails. Pressing her palms to her legs, she stared ahead.

He spoke again. "Don't you think it would be better if I said, 'Don't bite your nails, Suzie—or Gwendolyn—or Maisie'?"

"Yes. Much better. At least you'd be on Suzie, Gwendolyn and Maisie's backs. Not mine."

He flicked the turn signal as they glided onto Ninety-first Street. "Damn it. What's your first name?"

She smiled inwardly at the suddenness of his irritated outburst. Apparently there were ways to get under this man's smooth hide. "Here's the turnoff."

"A little long for a first name, isn't it?" he quipped as he steered the car into the wooded Landmark entryway and wound around the first row of stone-and-wood units.

"Why do you care what my first name is?"

"Damned if I know," he mumbled as he pulled to a stop before her—their—piggyback condos, situated in the most secluded corner of the development among a dense stand of oaks.

Turning the rumbling motor off, he reached across in front of her. "I know how I'll find out your name." He opened the glove compartment and pulled out a TU staff dictionary. "I'll do it the easy way."

She started to pull the book from him, but he took her wrist. "Oh, no, you don't. You read about me, I'm going to read about you."

When he released her arm to turn the pages, she didn't protest further. The fun had gone out of it. After all, if they were going to be neighbors for five months, he probably would have to know her first name sooner or later. Sometime she might need him to

collect her mail, feed her pets—if she ever got pets—
or let her hide in his closet during tornado alerts.
Usually, favors like that required people to be on a
first-name basis—especially when crouching together
in a closet. She frowned. On second thought, what
were the odds of being hit by a tornado—not really
that high. She'd lived in Oklahoma all her life and
never even seen one. For the time being, she decided
to shut out of her mind the idea of sharing a space as
small as a closet with this man.

While he flipped to the Ts, she let her eyes drift to
the open glove compartment. Without much interest
she began to catalog the contents—a pair of leather
driving gloves, a small folder of papers, probably car
registration and proof of insurance, a distributor cap,
a tube of lip balm . . .

Her eyes jerked back to the round plastic object. A
distributor cap! She'd learned what they looked like
when she took a course last year at TU called Lady,
Know Your Car. What was he doing with a distributor cap in his glove compartment? She picked it up and
fingered it. How odd that it looked so much like the
funny little one on her decrepit old car. It even had the
L-shaped scratch on it that hers had gotten when she'd
dropped a wrench on it. . . .

"Cara!" He slapped the book on the steering wheel.
"Cara Torrence." He looked down at her, a trium-
phant smile revealing glistening teeth. "I—"

"Why you! What did you think you'd accomplish
by that?" Fuming, more angry than she could ever
remember being in her life, she let out a guttural wail.

"Here! This is for the inconvenience!" Her distributor-cap-filled palm slammed into his lap.

Her eyes widened when she realized she'd missed her target. She'd meant to slap the book from his hand. His eyes widened, too. And his handsome features, frozen in shock, mirrored her stunned expression. Words of apology quivered on her lips for an instant, before her anger once again took charge. Clamping her jaws tight, she spun away, yanked on the door handle and jumped out of the car, leaving Martin Dante staring after her. The last sound she heard was a low moan as he hunched forward to rest his forehead on the steering wheel.

The book dropped from his fingers and fell between the bucket seats. He closed his eyes, muttering a low curse with the pain in his groin. What the hell was wrong with the woman? Was she crazy? Where had she gotten the brass knuckles she'd hit him with?

This Cara Torrence was a strange case—unquestionably mental. Why would anyone get so angry just because he'd looked up her name? Under his breath he gritted. "Cara—Cara Torrence." He shook his head, completely baffled. After another moment, he was able to straighten, open his door and slowly get out.

Chapter Three

Cara stepped out of her car into a stiff, warm breeze. She stood and stretched, inhaling the fresh air. It was going to be a beautiful Fourth of July. Maybe today's festivities would help her get her mind off the other night. For three days she'd felt rotten about where she'd accidentally hit Martin Dante with her distributor cap. If he hadn't turned at just that moment...

She closed her eyes to blot out the memory of his face. What a horrible thing to do to a man! Even she, in her worst moments, had never considered doing such a thing.

To rationalize that stealing her distributor cap had been his dirty trick in the first place, and anything he got he deserved, didn't make the memory of the pain she'd caused him any easier. She hadn't seen Martin since. That was a blessing. Maybe he was avoiding her with as much resolve as she had been avoiding him.

The billowing snap of a large banner at the entrance of Bell's Amusement Park caught her attention and she turned to squint up into the late-morning sunshine to read, "Meet Donnelly Wakefield, Oklahoma's Choice for Governor."

A gust of wind swirled the hem of her white cotton dress, lifting the multitucked fabric to reveal a hint of thigh. Pressing the air out of her skirt, she walked toward the amusement park entrance to join the crowd of Tulsans who were coming to meet the young gubernatorial candidate, feast on barbecued venison and enjoy discounted rides at this campaign celebration.

Tossing her head, she cleared her eyes of wind-tossled curls, sternly telling herself she would not dwell on Martin Dante any longer. She wove her way through the noisy merrymakers toward the Exposition Building where Donnelly Wakefield was to meet his Tulsa supporters later in the day.

She quickened her step. Raleigh was already there. It had been several weeks since Cara had seen her little sister, and she looked forward to the visit—though it was sure to be a harried one, since Raleigh was on duty as Donnelly's campaign manager.

She looked at her watch. It was nearly eleven. The Expo Building's side entrance was open, and the sound of a country band beckoned. She walked into the comparative darkness and squinted, looking about the cavernous hall. A catering service was setting up long tables, and two never-ending buffet lines. She could smell the barbecue, and realized with some surprise that she was hungry. She'd never tasted venison, and when Raleigh had told her about the menu she had groaned and vowed, with martyred firmness, that she never would. But now, she wasn't so sure.

"Cara! Caaaarrrraaa!"

Hearing her name called in the familiar soprano, she whirled to see her smiling little sister waving and walking toward her from the direction of the red-white-and-blue decorated platform where the band strummed a laid-back rendition of "Oklahoma."

Cara grinned at her sister. Marriage to Evan Younger had not hurt her one bit. She was radiant. And her choice of clothes was becoming positively classic. She was wearing a lean suit, tailored to show off her new-found sleekness. The off-white silk was detailed elegantly with soft, double-pleated lapels and welt pockets. Her hair, the same dark blond as Cara's, was pulled back and fastened at the crown of her head, flowing in soft curls to her shoulders. Her ears were touched tastefully with black onyx, and the onyx choker about her neck contrasted nicely with the deep V opening of her white suit jacket. The sophisticated cut of the jacket attractively showed off Raleigh's full figure—a figure that Cara tried hard not to envy.

Cara shook her head, but her smile was approving. "Is this the little kid who swore she'd never wear white because it got dirty too easily and made her look fat?"

Raleigh laughed. "Hi, Curly." She slid her hazel eyes over the taller woman. "For an exercise nut, you don't look so bad yourself." Taking Cara's hand, she led her toward the stage. "Donnelly should be here in about half an hour. He called just before they left the pancake breakfast in Oklahoma City.''

Cara's grin faded as she looked down at her sister's profile. There was a slightly drawn look there now, and she studied it for a moment without comment. As Raleigh pointed toward a door in the back wall, Cara ventured, ''Say, what's wrong? Is our candidate trailing a distant third, or something?''

''No—no, Donnelly's showing strong progress all over the state.'' But her sigh was audible as she nodded for Cara to precede her into the small office.

Once inside, Cara moved across the tile floor to a tweedy sofa and sat down. ''Well, then, why the tiny little worry lines? If they get any deeper, I'll be forced to start introducing you as my older sister.''

Raleigh's smile was melancholy as she took a seat on the other end of the small sectional. They faced each other, hazel eyes looking directly into hazel. They were sisters, and both of them knew that there was no point in kidding about their feelings.

Raleigh pushed off her white kid shoes and curled her feet up under her hips, twisting to face Cara more directly. The confident facade melted away as she leaned her elbow on the back of the couch and rested her cheek in her palm. Her smile was weary. ''Politics can make you old, I guess. Right now, we're finally feeling like we're getting an edge on the other two candidates running against us in the primary.'' She shrugged. ''But there's still the huge 'Incumbent Andrew Mathison' mountain to climb. Sometimes I feel like we're beating our heads against granite when I think about what's ahead.''

Cara couldn't help but notice how lovely her sister was, even in this solemn repose. Maybe she was even more lovely this way. It was funny how the Torrence sisters so rarely let their guard down to anyone except each other.

Her heart went out to her little sister, and Cara put out a consoling hand, touching Raleigh's knee. "Listen, Ral. It's only July. And remember, Donnelly Wakefield may be the new kid on the block, but he's the crusading kid. There's plenty of time between now and November for the voters to discover that he's what Oklahoma needs."

Raleigh lifted her eyes to Cara again. "I know. And I hope you're right. Donnelly deserves this chance—he could do so much for this state!"

Cara smiled. "You're telling me? Why do you think I'm your number-one volunteer?" She cocked her head toward the door. "Speaking of that, what did you want me to do here today? Maybe I could slip into my Ms. How-a-ya outfit and kiss some babies?"

Raleigh dropped her hand from her cheek and laughed. "Do you have that crazy outfit here?"

"In the car. I'm meeting my class at the River Parks at four o'clock. This is a new group, and they haven't clowned in public yet. I figured the Fourth of July would be a great time—people will be in a festive mood and love to see clowns."

Raleigh nodded. "Someday I'm going to do that with you—maybe after this election is over. I need a good laugh."

"Speaking of a good laugh, how's Evan?"

Raleigh's eyes lit like sparklers. "He's wonderful. Right now he's entertaining a group of kids from the Tulsa Boys' Home. When he found out they were here, he took them on—sort of a humanitarian project." She cast her eyes down to her lap, her cheeks flushing in uncharacteristic shyness. "Kind of like I was."

Cara laughed. "Sure. You were such a loser when he met you."

When Raleigh looked back up, her expression was serious. That surprised Cara. She'd been kidding when she'd called her sister a loser.

Raleigh lifted her chin, answering softly. "Maybe I was, but not anymore. I have Evan." She stood and straightened her skirt. "You should get so lucky someday."

Cara stood, too. "Luck isn't the word I'd use. But it does my old heart good to see that marriage was right for you, at least."

A loud knock rattled the door, drawing both pairs of eyes. "Yes?" Raleigh asked, quickly slipping into her shoes.

"I was just wondering if there might be a beautiful girl in a white dress in there?"

Both Cara and Raleigh smiled at the sound of Evan's teasing voice. Cara was first to answer. "Yes, darling. But your wife's in here, too, so fight the urge to run into my arms."

His laugh accompanied the opening of the door. Cara noticed that he looked the same as always, casually stylish, in a woven tattersall shirt and gray corduroy pants. "Cara." He acknowledged her with a wave as he strode to Raleigh and brushed her lips with a loving kiss. Turning to Cara, he lightly brushed her cheek with a kiss. "Lovely as ever—and in a dress, yet."

Cara feigned annoyance. "I guess it's true what they say. You can pick your friends but you can't pick your family." Then with a genuine smile she hugged him warmly.

She let go of him and stepped back. He was shaking his head at her. "I can't wait to meet the gladiator that walks into the lion's den to face you and comes out with a purring kitten in his arms."

Cara liked Evan more than she liked any man she knew. But every time he made a remark like that, she felt herself tense for battle. She didn't want to fight with Evan. He wanted only to help people. His remark was not meant to hurt her, it was just a sort of minipsychoanalysis. After all, he was a psychologist for the Tulsa Police Department.

Raleigh seemed to sense Cara's tensed hesitation, and stepped in. "Younger—" she took his elbow "—if you think I was a hard case, you haven't seen anything until you tangle with my sister—at least on the subject of men."

Her look was so adoring and his so loving, that Cara felt a strange pang of something like jealousy when she watched them gaze at each other for that quiet moment.

Jealousy? Never. She shook off the feeling, forcing a laugh. "Besides, Evan, when Raleigh stole you from your cradle, there just wasn't a male left worth having—child or adult. Certainly you can understand how all other guys seem so unpalatable next to you."

Evan snorted. "I'd be a fool to argue that." He pulled his wife beneath one arm and moved to swing the other about Cara's shoulders. "How's this? I won't mention your staggering misconceptions about men, if you keep off the subject of my tender age."

"Baby brother, you've got yourself a deal—until the next time, of course." A faint smile quirked at her lips. She knew as well as he did that those were their two favorite subjects, and because they loved each other, they could forever get away with their friendly sparring.

The band was strumming a country rendition of "The Star Spangled Banner" when they stepped out of the office, and Evan chuckled. "Francis Scott Key—on the range."

The women laughed, and Raleigh put her arm around his waist as she turned to Cara. "About the clown suit. I didn't ask you to come today to work, Curly, I just want friendly faces around—friendly, pretty faces."

"Aha!" Evan exclaimed. "That's why I was invited."

"She said pretty faces. You're here on a sympathy pass 'cause you know the boss," Cara quipped.

Evan looked down at her, an amused frown pursing his lips. "I'd say that cease-fire lasted about thirty seconds, old lady. What's your guess?"

She smiled blandly. "Twenty-six seconds, I make it."

"My mistake." He grunted out a chuckle. "But for the record, Cara, don't tell me that after all the time we've known each other, you've missed the fact that I am terribly attractive?''

She closed her eyes in exaggerated disbelief. "The kid is right, for once. The attractive part, I missed. But can you really blame me?''

Evan looked overly thoughtful. "You're probably right. I've heard that older people tend to have bad eyesight.''

As Cara opened her mouth to retort, Raleigh interjected, "Would you mind stuffing a couple of socks in it for now? I'd like to have my nervous breakdown without being sidetracked.''

She reached across her husband to tug on Cara's sleeve. "As for you and your question about helping—I was hoping you would be charming and mingle for as long as you can before you have to go clown.''

"Oh!'' Evan pretended horror. "Don't tell me you're going to allow that crazy Miss What-is-it out again without a keeper?''

"How-a-ya.'' Cara corrected him with a dip of her brows.

"I'm just fine—except for a curly-headed pain in the neck. Thanks for asking.'' He was loving his little joke, and Cara couldn't help but laugh at being so easily maneuvered into it.

"Oh!''

Cara and Evan turned to look at Raleigh's animated expression. Apparently so preoccupied with her job, Raleigh hadn't heard their last exchange. "There is one other thing I'd forgotten about, Cara. You really could help me out tomorrow. I'm supposed to pick up some demographic updates from the computer firm that's handling the election tactics for us, and I can't. I'll be with Donnelly taping a television spot, and Jenny has picked this week to have her baby. Robin is out with strep throat and—''

Cara raised a hand. "Hold it, kid. I get the picture. You're in luck. I've given my sociology classes a free day tomorrow to go to the library and do research. I'm available all day. I'll pick 'em up. Where and when?''

Raleigh smiled. "Thanks. Adams Building. Downtown. Dante Data Corporation has the eighth floor. Martin was expecting me about eleven but if that's a bad time for you, just call and tell him when you can come in.''

Cara's smile faded, and she felt her throat go dry. Her face must have gone gray and stony if Raleigh's widened eyes could tell anything. "Why, Cara, what's wrong? You look like you've just seen the devil.''

Cara fought the urge to shout out that she had not only seen him—she'd rendered him momentarily inoperative. "I . . . I . . .'' She didn't want to talk about how she happened to know Martin Dante. Especially when she was working so hard at blocking her entire association with him out of her mind. With a few scratchy swallows, she shook off the anger and shock his name had precipitated, and attempted to smile. "Sorry, Ral, it's nothing—just a headache coming on.''

Raleigh's face registered concern. "Oh? I hope you're not coming down with strep, too.''

Cara tried valiantly to turn her grimace into a smile. She couldn't manage to do it and look Raleigh straight in the eye, too. Dropping her gaze to her sandals, she assured her sister. "Oh, no. I'm fine. I'll get those charts for you." An idea struck her that might save her from having to see Martin. "Come to think of it," she lied, "I'll need to be in my office in the morning, so I won't be able to pick up the charts until twelve-thirty or thereabouts. Would you mind calling Mr. Dante and suggesting that he leave the information with his secretary? That way, I won't have to bother him at all."

Raleigh's brows puckered. "Well, sure, I guess I could arrange it. But you ought to meet Martin. He's a fine man. I mean, anyone who could be trusted to help both parties in a hot election year has to be well respected." Raleigh whispered across Evan's chest, "Besides, he's a hunk."

"I heard that." Evan cleared his throat, and curled his arm tighter about Raleigh's neck, cupping her chin with his fingers. "You forgot to say he's a clear second to your husband."

Raleigh smiled up at him, grazing his jaw with her lips. Her murmur was just loud enough for Cara to hear, as she repeated his words, "Martin Dante is a hunk, but a clear second to my husband."

Cara looked away, trying to push all thoughts of Martin Dante out of her mind. Her eyes traveled to the open side entrance. A familiar silhouette caught her eye and she smiled, relieved to be able to change the subject. "Our candidate has arrived. It's time to start slinging those Bambi burgers."

Raleigh laughed. "Curly, if you dare call this multithousand-dollar promotional lunch Bambi burgers in front of our contributors, I'll strangle you."

"Kidding." Cara slanted a teasing smile toward her sister. "Just kidding. I'll be the perfect campaign manager's sister, I promise."

Evan's deep chuckle was not reassuring.

Even considering the deer meat, Cara felt that the packed tables and resounding applause for Donnelly's speech had made for a successful campaign lunch. She just hoped that the polls in the coming weeks would reflect that success—both for Donnelly's sake and for Raleigh's.

Now it was after four o'clock, and Cara, or Ms. How-a-ya, postured and loped along the River Parks grounds in the shade of towering oaks. Her clowns had been briefed and set free amid the milling Fourth of July celebrators.

One young man had come as a flamboyantly dressed jogger with a painted face depicting extreme exhaustion and pain. Moments ago, he had set off down the winding jogging path, a bouquet of balloons billowing out from his belt. He'd had each balloon imprinted with the phrase, Boston Marathon or Bust. She smiled at his ingenuity. That was the wonderful thing about this clowning project in the self-discovery class—in the five years she'd taught it, she never ceased to be amazed at the breadth of the participants' originality and the galaxy of variations in their conceptions of what was humorously bizarre.

Proud of her pupils, Cara couldn't stifle a smile as she surveyed the troupe of nine novice clowns. They were spreading out along the bank of the Arkansas River entertaining the crowd of Independence Day celebrators as they picnicked and waited for the traditional fireworks extravaganza.

Agatha, an elderly bookkeeper, was clad in a tattered wedding gown and carried a bouquet of wilted weeds. Her gray hair was combed in webby disarray. A bit off center, a piece of fishnet was secured to a plastic rose. Her lined face was painted to depict angelic innocence, and every man who happened to wander by was immediately accosted by this petite bride, pretending to search for a long-lost groom.

More than once a man, caught unawares, would show surprise at being taken in tow and dragged toward some imaginary chapel. But never once did any man disengage himself without a good-natured smile, and maybe even a bended-knee proposal. These were the spontaneous things that made clowning so fulfilling—sharing impulsive, friendly laughter with a stranger.

Cara's clowns were going their own way—without benefit of identity or words—to get in touch with themselves by going beyond their self-image, and to have fun.

She looked at her watch. They were to meet in one hour. Now she, too, was on her own.

It was hot. Even now, at four-thirty, the temperature hovered at ninety. She spotted a drinking fountain and began clowning in the general direction of water. Two small children rushed up to her, laughing and squealing and tugging on her grass skirt. Feigning panic, she jumped onto one end of a concrete picnic table. With a foot held high, she posed, looking down at the two children, her arms thrown wide, her mouth opened in a pantomimed scream.

She was amused to note that the children's expressions were now gap-mouthed. It would have been a good guess that they were surprised to learn of their awesome power to provoke terror in the heart of this sad lady jester.

"G-girl?" The older of the two children, a girl of about six, shook her curly head, reassuringly. "You don't have to be scared. We wasn't gonna hurt ya."

Cara's sad mask closed in a questioning frown.

"Uh-uh." The younger child, a blond boy, frowned too. "We were kidding." He held up a chubby hand. "Come down. Your mommy'll swat ya for standin' on the table."

Cara made a wide-eyed play at moving her stare to her one foot, balanced on the table, as though she had never considered what her mother might say.

"Yes, do get down, Ms. How-a-ya, those feet are not very appetizing."

Cara froze—her blood froze, her purple hair froze, even her skirt froze in the sudden stillness. That voice! It couldn't be!

Very slowly, she lowered her suspended foot and turned around to convince herself that she must be wrong. Martin Dante would not lower himself to come to a public park where ordinary people were celebrating the Fourth of July. Surely he was at Arrowhead Country Club or some such elite place roasting gold-plated marshmallows and drinking ambrosia out of silver goblets.

Wrong. When hazel eyes slammed into mercury-blue, she felt as though she'd just slid into ice water. He, however, was unmoved. Lounging casually at the other end of the table, a cola in one hand, Martin looked very preppy in a white sport shirt, white tennis shorts, tennis shoes and socks so pristine she was sure they'd never seen a court.

Next to him, looking up and smiling at Cara's antics, was an attractive brunette dressed in a pink sundress with lace straps. The tanned woman was shaking her head reassuringly. "Don't worry about it, miss. He's only kidding. You're wonderful."

Cara spun around on the tabletop, turning to face them. No matter how badly she wanted to run, it wasn't possible. There might have been cowardly clowns in the world, but Cara Torrence was not one of them. With that brave vow stiffening her spine, she confronted the dastardly Mr. Dante. She'd show him! If he didn't like the way she'd acted in the coffee shop the other night, he'd hate what she was about to do! With a pert curtsy to the young woman's compliment, she took a swivel-hipped step toward them, patting her purple pigtails coquettishly. But before she could take one more undulating step, Martin moved away from his companion. Then, to Cara's astonishment, he poured his cola down the front of his shirt, wadded the plastic cup and tossed it into a nearby trash container. Amid surprised laughter, he took his gaping young companion by the hand. Saluting Cara with a scowling nod, he said simply, "Thanks, but I'd rather do it myself."

"Hey, I like playin' racquetball in the morning. Get's your blood goin', don't it?" Bobby stretched, inhaling, as he walked off the court with Martin. "By the way, how was your Fourth, yesterday? Didn't see ya at the Arrowhead party."

"I went to the River Parks with a date. And, on the whole, it was very nice."

Bobby pushed the locker room door open and cocked his friend a sidelong look. "On the whole? Who'd you go with—Miss third-place America? Or maybe, was it someone else we both know?"

Martin eyed his friend with half-lowered lids. "Would you quit referring to her that way? She's a very attractive woman. And I hope to heaven I'll never have a date with someone we both know. Ever since the fifth grade, there's been only one thing about you I've really hated—and I mean besides your perverted sense of humor—that's your demented curiosity about the women I date." He turned away and pulled his mesh T-shirt over his head.

Martin heard Bobby's racquetball shoes drop into the bottom of his locker one at a time before he turned around again to face his friend. Bobby was watching him rather oddly, and there was a crooked smile parting his lips. "I repeat, was it the very attractive Miss A., or somebody else?"

"Okay, Dunlap." Impatience laced Martin's tone. "Spill it."

Bobby snorted and reached up to scratch his head. "Nothin' to spill. I'm waitin' for you to spill something to me."

Martin pursed his lips in a frown. "What do you think I could possibly have to tell you?"

Bobby shrugged out of his green cotton shirt. "Oh, maybe a little somethin' about the other night and a fair damsel in distress."

Martin's frown deepened in confusion. "Your point?"

Bobby unsnapped his shorts and slipped them down over his long legs before sitting down to take off his socks. "The date I arranged for you, old buddy." He bent to pull his socks off. "The fair Ms. Torrence and her crippled car."

"What do you mean you arranged a date for me with Cara?" He winced at the sound of her name.

"Cara!" Bobby lifted his legs and swiveled on the bench to face Martin. "Well, that puts you way out in front of the field, man—if she lets you call her Cara! Looks like you owe me somethin' for settin' this deal up."

"You? You had something to do with our meeting?" Martin's square jaw began to flex. He cringed inwardly, forced to recall the odd duck of a professor. It was a shame that such a lunatic personality had been packaged in such an attractive body.

Losing all interest in getting to the Exchange Bank board meeting he was chairing in a half hour, he sat down on the bench and rested an elbow on his knee. His chin settled on a fist. "This had better be damn good, Dunlap. That woman has caused me considerable pain, and before I kill you, I'd like to know what lousy practical joke of yours is finally going to leave your blood on my hands.''

Ignoring Martin's threatening tone, Bobby sat back, resting his hands on the bench. His eyes narrowed with his devilish smile. ''Soooooo! She's scalped you, too!'' He elbowed Martin in the ribs. ''Tell me, Dante, with that black and silver glory of yours hangin' from her belt, do you still think you'd like to run with interestin' women, or is it enough for you to just date 'beautiful and perfect' ladies from now on?'' He jumped up and swaggered over to the stack of thick white towels, laughing. Pulling off his undershorts, he wrapped the towel around his sparse middle. ''Just for the record, what did she do to you?''

Ignoring Bobby's gibes, Martin sat up, folding his arms before his chest. ''You're just putting off the inevitable. Confess and take your medicine like a brave fool. I'll help you start.''

His frown deepened as he recalled his first sight of Cara Torrence in the parking lot. It seemed incredible now, in the face of what had happened, that he'd been immediately attracted to the woman. Looking back, he realized that his safest course would have been to turn and run the minute she'd clipped her car with her fist.

Shrugging off the memory, he coaxed tiredly, ''Somehow you got her car disabled so that she'd have to ask me for a ride, didn't you.'' It wasn't a question.

''Check—took out her distributor cap.'' Bobby flipped open the white curtain and stepped into the shower stall. "I'm kinda surprised you haven't found it. I put it in your glove compart—" Bobby found his ability to speak and his forward motion halted by a heavy hand biting painfully into his shoulder.

"Her distributor cap! You put her distributor cap in my glove compartment?" Now it was all starting to fit together—why Cara Torrence had suddenly gone out of her mind! She'd found the cap in his glove compartment. Then she'd assumed God knows what and hit him with it!

"And like a fool I told you where I keep a magne-tized key on my car frame," Martin growled, trem-bling to keep from pulverizing his friend on the spot. "Bobby, this time you've really done it! Lord, I thought she was the unbalanced one!" Dropping his hand listlessly to his side, he groaned out a tired breath. "Damn it, you dumb cowboy, because of you, I owe her one hell of an apology."

Bobby turned back to see Martin's stricken expres-sion, and took a safeguarding step backward as he spoke. "Why bother? She'll just kick you before you can get within apologizing distance. Forget about her and go back to dating perfect Miss America types. Leave Cara Torrence to the lion tamers of the world. Face it, Dante, my boy, you're not the 'fire-eater' type—she's too spicy a diet for a button-down con-servative like you."

Martin pursed his lips in an irritated frown. "You make her sound like a wild boar."

Bobby laughed. "Were you bored?"

Martin snorted, but said nothing.

"I doubt if a man has ever even yawned in her presence—groaned, bled and crumpled into a broken heap, yes—but never yawned. Why, I've heard tell that she's cut off more men at the knees than any 'gator in the Everglades."

Martin turned away, "That's ridiculous. She's just a woman—not even a very big one. And now that I know why she was so angry the other night, I can understand most of her erratic behavior." Envisioning her clown face, he couldn't help but include the qualifying "most."

The very fact that she became a clown on frequent occasions proved that she was odd. It was a little disconcerting to realize that this strangeness of hers was so powerful it had actually rubbed off on him. He winced inwardly at the memory of how he'd dumped his own drink on himself. That unexpected behavior bothered him when he allowed himself to think about it.

But just because she was unconventional in her lifestyle, and just because her radical actions made some part of his brain start jangling "tilt," she didn't deserve the maniac label he'd filed her away under. "Actually, Bobby, you're right. She's not boring."

"Yeah? What does that mean—you plannin' to get back into the cage with her?"

Martin lifted a foot to the bench and began to untie his racquetball shoe with an irritated pull on the laces. "It means only that I plan to apologize to the woman. I don't intend for her to think I'm a low, conniving womanizer who'd stoop to any ploy to get her in his clutches."

Bobby whistled. "Is that what she thinks? Hell, man, I thought she'd be flattered that you'd go to such lengths to meet her."

"You probably would, Dunlap. But then you're a jerk."

"It's a good thing you're my best friend, Dante. I don't let anybody but my best friend and my mother call me that."

Bobby's unbothered response only served to irritate Martin further. "Take your shower." He sat down and pulled off his shoes, raising his voice so that Bobby could hear him over the running water. "As far as the idea of actually asking her out, I don't think so." He was recalling the Fourth of July, seeing Cara leap onto the table that he and Belinda were sharing. Still, there was something very intriguing about her; maybe it was the very fact that she was so damned unpredictable.

Bobby shouted in a gurgled distortion of the human voice. "Good. I bet you a hundred bucks she'd tell you to drop dead if you asked her out—five hundred she'd hit your face if you tried to get her in bed."

Martin scowled at the curtain. "I don't bet on things like that."

Laughter filled the locker room for an instant before Bobby began to choke from inhaling the shower spray. After a few moments of listening to Bobby struggle for life, Martin wasn't sure he was pleased to hear that his friend had won the battle. Bobby said, needling him, "Afraid to lose a few bucks oh—alleged—great lover?"

"Shut up," Martin growled.

"I'm to take that as a yes, then?"

"Take it for whatever you want."

Bobby stepped out of the shower, his curly hair dripping. As he wrapped his towel about his waist, he tossed his head, whipping the hair back out of his eyes. "Okay loverboy. But I'm still bettin' the lady will flatten you, just to be able to say 'I told you so.'" He grabbed another towel and fluffed his hair. "And to show you what a sport I am, if you do get the lady in bed, I'll fork over five hundred bucks to you, anyway."

Martin shrugged in a careless dismissal; his naked torso dipped gracefully as he grabbed a towel and headed toward the showers. For some reason his face grew hot, and he could feel sweat break out on his chest and back. Get Cara Torrence—that unpredictable hellcat—in bed? The vision of her slender body lying next to him was tempting, he had to admit. But was a tumble with her worth the trouble?

He felt a rush of desire in his groin. Hell, it was worth a trip to Hades and back. But if he did get her in his bed, Bobby Dunlap would never know it. That was not the way Martin operated.

Hoping Bobby could not see the physical effect his fantasy of Cara Torrence was having on him, Martin attempted nonchalance as he tossed the towel over his shoulder and yanked open the curtain of a stall. Without looking over his back to assure himself that Bobby could not have noticed anything amiss, he gritted out, "Go to hell, Dunlap—and take your money with you."

Chapter Four

Martin looked at his watch and muttered a curse. The elevator doors opened onto the eighth floor of the Adams Building, and he hurried out into an alcove of understated elegance. The walls and plush carpet were a soft shell color, a neutral and even-textured backdrop for the antique and brass accessories that warmed the entrance to Dante Data Corporation. Brass lettering beside the double doors left no doubt as to the name of the company or its president.

Martin strode briskly through the doors, his mind on his eleven o'clock appointment with Raleigh Younger. He was already fifteen minutes late. The bank meeting had taken longer than he had anticipated, and it irritated him to be late. It was something he didn't abide in others, and found inexcusable in himself.

The bright reception area was the same shell tone as the exterior entry. Original paintings in various media and styles, all common in their earthy tones, warmed the walls. The furnishings were an aesthetic contrast of angles and textures, a tasteful mixing of contemporary design and elegant antiques.

Leonora Walters, his secretary, stood, brushing back her sleek, graying hair. Leo's hair was always in place, but she was forever pressing it down as though she believed it to be in a constant state of disarray.

"Martin." Leo's glasses hung from a silver chain about her neck and she often made a great show of reading her boss's messages by propping the glasses over her thin nose, as she was doing now. "Mrs. Younger called early on, concerning her eleven o'clock appointment. She's sending someone else for the charts—a Ms. Torrence. She said that this Ms. Torrence would come in during the noon hour. Her suggestion was that you leave the information with me to relay to her, so as not to disturb your appointment schedule."

Martin's smile faded. "Ms. Torrence?" he asked. "Did Raleigh by any chance give you a first name?" He doubted by any stretch of the imagination that it could possibly be—

"Cara, I believe."

His brows came together as he made the connection.

Professor Cara Torrence was Raleigh Torrence Younger's sister. He hadn't thought about it before, but there was a definite family resemblance. For some reason, Raleigh was sending the reluctant professor to see him—probably kicking and protesting all the way. He'd bet his last dollar that she hadn't volunteered. The "leave the information with the secretary" line was proof of that. Cara was doing this as a very large family favor, and would never have agreed to come if it hadn't been important to Raleigh.

Apparently Cara was a Donnelly Wakefield fan. That wouldn't be hard to understand even if her sister hadn't been working for him. Wakefield was handsome, single and, by all reports, moving up rapidly in the political scene. What woman wouldn't be attracted to a man like that? Martin's brows knit further. Could there be something serious going on between the candidate and the clown? Why not? Wakefield didn't have a Bobby Dunlap to make him look like a creep.

And Martin Dante knew he was just that in Cara's eyes. He would have had to be as thick as an oilman's wallet not to notice that she had been avoiding him at the condominium. Whatever her reasons for coming, she'd have to see him now. At least he would have his opportunity to apologize.

With that positive thought, he nodded, turning his attention back to Leo. "Anything else?"

"Yes. You had several other phone calls—and your car won't be ready until six." She handed him a stack of messages.

"Thanks, Leo." He took them without interest. "About the demographics for the Wakefield campaign..." He fingered the metal sculpture on the edge of his secretary's desk. "There are several things I need to explain to Ms. Torrence, and she may have questions." Leo was listening attentively, her glasses now dangling down the front of her blouse. "Might as well tell the programmers I'll take a look at their computations now. And at noon I'll have lunch in my office."

Leo sat down and lifted the receiver of her phone. With a pencil eraser poised over the buttons, she said, "Yes sir. And about lunch, something from Tules, downstairs?"

"Something light." He stopped, his hand on his brass doorknob, and turned back. "Make that for two."

The door of his office closed behind him as he walked to his massive desk, which was framed by a wall of long windows. The walls in his office were wood paneled and lined with bookshelves, a dark contrast to the reception area.

The thing that made Martin's office stand out from other company presidents' plush surroundings was the scattering of modular computer equipment.

A printer was rat-tat-tatting and spitting out sheet after sheet of continuous-form paper when Martin's intercom drew his attention from the printouts. Switching off the printer, he strode to the desk and pressed the intercom button. "Yes?"

"Ms. Torrence to see you, sir." He quirked a brow to hear Cara's hushed voice behind his secretary's. She was whispering a strong denial of any need to see him. Feeling an odd combination of irritation and amusement, he directed, "Send her in, Leo. And you may go on to lunch now."

"Yes, sir."

Martin reached over and turned off the computer. He was lounging casually against his desk when Leo pushed open his door, saying, "Really, Ms. Torrence, if he didn't think it was important, he would have left it with me."

Cara was certainly fighting this. For some reason, instead of being irritated by her antagonism, he found her resistence highly intriguing. He couldn't ever remember a woman working so hard not to be with him.

Cara appeared in the door. He didn't have to be a mind reader to know by her clamp-jawed expression that she was not delighted.

"Hello, Professor. Come in." He flashed a cordial smile and motioned toward a round table in the corner opposite the door. There were two leather chairs pushed up to it. When lunch was delivered Leonora had had it placed in his office. On the table was a pristine tablecloth and two place settings of silver. Two Mexican chef salads, one stemmed glass, one tumbler of water and a bottle of red wine awaited someone's pleasure. He didn't give her much time to wonder whose. "I hope you haven't eaten."

Cara stared at the table, and then at Martin Dante. She hadn't, but she had no intention of eating with him. "Why...I...." She decided to lie. "Actually, I was planning to meet someone later."

Martin's look was doubtful as he took in her jogging suit and shoes. "I trust you are dining somewhere casual. McDonald's perhaps?"

She stiffened. What business was it of his where she chose to eat? Feeling that McDonald's needed no defense from her, she decided to be fleet of both explanation and foot—get the charts and get out! Lifting a regal chin, she feigned seriousness. "Actually I'm dining at the Petroleum Club. I have a dress on under this. Now if you'll just give me those charts—" She winced, feeling pain in her heel. Martin's iron maiden of a secretary was trying to close the door!

"Excuse me, Ms. Torrence, but I can't shut the door with your foot there." The door's vise grip on her mashed heel and Leo's tattling gave Cara but two choices. She could make a scene and scream that she had no intention of being shut in an office with Martin, or she could pretend surprise that her heel was being squeezed into a wedge, and step obediently inside. The scene idea was her first choice, but the pain in her foot won out over bravery, and she pulled it away.

Martin walked toward her, and she had to fight the urge to back into the just latched door. He suggested, "At least have some wine while I go over the results with you." He had taken her elbow and was leading her toward the table. She would have fought the trip more intensely if she hadn't been concentrating on not limping.

Her forearms came to rest on soft leather. She was sitting down. How did she get there? Jerking her eyes forward, she watched as Martin took the other seat. He didn't say anything further until he had poured her a glass of wine. Handing her the glass, he asked, "You aren't really going to meet anyone for lunch, are you?''

Caught off guard, she took the wine and cast her eyes around the room nervously. Taking a stalling sip, she found herself meeting his gaze directly over the rim. His eyes were very light, very clear. She lowered the glass and licked her lips.

''You aren't,'' he repeated. But without giving her time to answer, he went on. ''I know you think I'm some sort of twisted pervert and you hate the sight of me.''

She swallowed, dropping her hand from the glass to the tabletop. ''You flatter yourself, Mr. Dante. I don't think nearly so highly of you.''

With an almost imperceptible wince, he closed one eye. His smile was crooked and wry. ''Another good shot, Professor. That time, I think you got a little spit in my eye.''

For some reason, his injured good humour made her feel slightly guilty. Once again the urge to apologize for the other night flitted through her mind. Fighting it, she kept her expression aggressive, and said nothing.

Inclining his head, he indicated the table. ''This lunch is an apology for the other night. I'd like to explain, if you'll let me.''

She hadn't bargained for this turn of events. Crossing her arms before her warm-up top, she sat back. This was likely to be very inventive. Her shrug was meant to be one of disinterest. Nothing could have been further from the truth. She eyed him evenly. ''I don't have much time, Mr. Dante. I'm expecting a headache." She gritted the flippant remark out, fully expecting to get up and leave in the next few seconds. But until that time came, it might be interesting to hear what he had to say.

He leaned forward, placing his forearms on the table. "I didn't know that your distributor cap was in my car that night, nor how it got there, until this morning." He frowned. "A friend of mine with a rather—unique—sense of humor did it without my knowledge."

Cara's only move was the doubtful lift of one brow. "Mr. Dante, do I look like a fool to you?"

His sleepy gaze slid over her, and Cara thought she could see a sparkle of mirth beneath the dark lashes. "A woman who wears oversize shoes and fluorescent pigtails would do herself a favor never to ask that question."

"Don't try to weasel out of this by trying to put me on the defensive. You know what I mean. I don't believe that."

"I had some difficulty believing it myself." Martin's frown slowly faded, changing to a smile that was both endearing and apologetic. Touching his fork, he asked, "Will you join me? Tules makes some of the best Mexican food in town."

When she shook her head, he sat back, folding his arms across his chest. Now they were both sitting away from the table, like two stubborn bookends. He made no further move to eat. He just sat there, a determined expression on his face, watching her.

After a silent minute, she had to ask, "Well, even if there really were such a sick person, why would he or she put my distributor cap in your car? That makes no sense." She sat forward, her forearm brushing her goblet. It sloshed toward Martin, spilling wine onto his suit pants. Planting both palms on the table, Cara jumped to her feet. "Oh, no!"

Martin moved quickly, but not quickly enough to miss being doused. When he stood up, Cara had already bounded to his side and was dabbing at his lap with her linen napkin. "Oh, damn! Red wine is impossible to get out!" she moaned, dropping to her knees, and swiping furiously at the soaked fabric.

Martin gripped her wrist; his hold was as firm as his voice was husky. "What is it with you and my lap?" He pulled her to her feet. "Do you do this to all men, or have you singled me out for some reason?"

She'd been concentrating so hard on getting the wine stain out, she hadn't even thought about where it was located. She stammered, "Uh...I—" Clutching her napkin between fingers that had begun to shake, she closed her eyes, wishing fervently that when she opened them again she would be dead. Wishes being the untrustworthy things they were, she didn't die. Unless you could break out in a cold sweat post mortem she knew she was still very much alive.

A crazy, illogical rush of desire began to pulsate in her core, heating her all the way out to her flushed skin. The warmth generated was a tingling mixture of excitement and embarrassment. She didn't care to speculate which warmth took precedence over which.

Her eyes refused to settle on Martin's face, preferring to flit in aimless distress about the room as she defended herself. "I ... acted on impulse ... trying to help. So sue me."

Her eyes, in their frantic wanderings, finally fell victim to the pull of Martin's gaze, and settled there with the stupidity of a fly settling on flypaper. His eyes were clear and a bit too bright.

The hand that had pulled her to her feet slid up to her shoulder. "I guess that won't be necessary." He shook his head and met her eyes again. Sliding his other hand to her shoulder, he lowered his voice to a confidence. "If you'll accept my apology for the other night, I'll accept yours for the wine."

"Well..." Her voice sounded husky in her ears. She rubbed the outside of her arms. How could she feel so flushed and chilled at the same time? Trying to mask her discomfort, she jutted her chin, countering, "I don't know, Mr. Dante. I was caused a lot of embarrassment and inconvenience—"

With a low chuckle, he interjected. "So was I, or hadn't you noticed?"

She blanched, wanting to get out of there. "I ... I accept your apology." Pulling out of his hold, she mumbled, "Now, if you'll give me those charts, I'll be going."

"And leave me this way?"

"What way?"

He spread his arms. "Look at me."

"No thanks." Nothing or no one could get her to look down. Her lips grew pinched. "The charts, please." She held out a hand and was distressed to notice that her fingers were still trembling.

He shook his head. "I'll make a deal with you. There are a few new compilations in the data I made up for Raleigh. If you give me a ride to my condo, I'll explain the changes on the way. I have an appointment at Resource Sciences out near Seventy-first and Yale at three o'clock, and my car won't be ready until six. You'd be doing me a favor."

"What's wrong with your car?" She held up a halting hand. "Do I dare hope it's minus a distributor cap, too?"

His unrestrained laughter surprised her. "Nothing like that. I'm just having the tires rotated and the engine tuned."

"Too bad." She was avoiding the subject of the ride, hoping to divert him from it long enough to grab the charts and back out of the room. "How will you get back downtown to get your car tonight?"

"Taxi."

She had half a mind to suggest that a taxi could also get him to his condo, but that would have been petty. After all, she had been responsible for ruining his pants and she was heading home anyway. Her hesitation relayed her reluctance, but with a grim toss of her heavy mane of hair she acquiesced. "All right. I suppose I could drop you off."

"Good." He began to shrug out of his suit coat. "And call me Martin, or Mart, please. You make me feel like a freshman sociology student when you call me Mr. Dante." With the coat draped over his arm, masking the red stain on his beige linen pants, he motioned toward the large manila envelope marked

Wakefield. "If you get that, I'll be a gentleman and get the door."

Quickly, she took the envelope from his desk and tucked it under one arm. "Don't concern yourself about it, Martin. I'm not impressed by having doors opened for me."

"Oh?" With his hand poised on the knob, he paused. "I'm curious. Just what does impress you?" He dropped his hand, leaving the door closed.

She reached for the knob. "I'll tell you, but you won't like it." She eyed him levelly. "You're a man who's logical, always doing the correct thing. I bet you've never made a foolish move in your life—never followed your heart and damned the consequences." She pulled the door open and walked out, leaving Martin to enjoy the petulant sway of her hips as she thrust him a pointed gibe over her shoulder. "To be perfectly frank, Martin, I admire the sentimental fools of this world."

Cara sat in Martin's living room, not quite sure why she was still there—except that she planned to take his suit pants to the dry cleaners. She looked aimlessly around. The room was familiar. She'd been here several times before Rosie and Maury had moved. The living room was large and comfortably furnished for easygoing hospitality. She sat back on the long sofa that was arranged at a right angle to a matching love seat. Their brown-and-blue print upholstery was the genesis for the color scheme used in the kitchen and dining areas, too.

Floor-to-ceiling accessorizing, from the carved horse and antique sled to the children's chairs and baskets hung Shaker fashion on a pegged cornice, gave the room an individual style and warmth. On one side of the freestanding fireplace was an antique brass tub filled with firewood, in July merely an accent piece, bringing out the rustic quality of the weathered wood frame of the antique print that hung above it.

On the other side of the fireplace was something new—or rather new to the condominium, although it, too, was an antique of fine quality. It was an old oak-and-punched-aluminum pie safe. Curiosity had forced Cara to look inside, and she was surprised to see it contained a portable computer and printer, as well as an assortment of computer equipment such as paper, disks and manuals. She smiled, wondering if the cabinetmaker of some hundred and fifty odd years ago could have visualized that one day a mechanical brain would be housed in his pie safe.

"Well? What do you think?" Martin came out of the hall that led to the bedrooms, a burgundy-and-black-striped silk tie draped around his neck, falling on either side of his partially open shirtfront. He was dressed in a white wing-collared shirt and black slacks. Over his arm he carried a burgundy blazer with the unmistakable slub of rich silk. With the precision of an engineer, he folded the jacket over the back of the love seat before buttoning the shirt collar at his neck and slipping the tie into place. As he looped a knot in the tie, he went on conversationally, "You haven't asked a single question about the charts. I hope that means my explanations have been adequate."

She picked up the computer printouts that she had quit examining a good five minutes ago. "I think I understand everything."

"You make my job too easy." He smiled as he looked down at the oval coffee table where he had previously set a bucket of ice and two glasses. "I forgot to fix you that drink. You must think I'm a terrible host." He lifted both glasses and walked toward the kitchen door. "What would you like—Gatorade or water?"

"You're kidding."

His low laugh echoed in the kitchen. "I would never kid a woman who insists on perfect frankness."

"Water, then." She stood up to follow him. "Gatorade always gives me an urge to tackle quarterbacks."

"Lucky quarterbacks."

She heard his low rejoinder, but decided to ignore it as she rounded the doorjamb into a kitchen geared to cater a feast. The old-world warmth of the beamed ceiling combined with the advantages of recessed lighting, the twelve-foot-long work center with two self-venting grill rangers, the double sink, the rustically decorated banks of drawers and floor-to-ceiling storage cabinets—all these features combined both the best of the old and the new.

Cara joined Martin beside the mushroom-colored refrigerator as he filled the glasses with water from the dispenser in the door. "You know, most single men who invite me in for a drink don't mean water."

He turned to her, his smile friendly. "Remember, I offered you Gatorade, too."

She took the glass, lowering her eyes to the ice cubes that swirled in the clear liquid. "Very funny."

"You're welcome."

Her lashes fluttered back up to meet his teasing gaze. "Okay. Thanks." Her lips, behind the lifted glass, became a tentative smile. Maybe he really hadn't taken her distributor cap. After all, once very long ago she'd witnessed the results of another practical joke played on him. For some reason, standing here in his kitchen, looking up into his easy smile, she wanted it to be true.

He wasted no time in absorbing the possibilities reflected in her small smile. There was an explosive change in his eyes. Something was going to happen. She stilled, unable to take the sip from the glass she held poised at her lips. Then, removing the decision from her completely, he lifted the glass from her hand and placed it, as well as his own, on the counter top.

The unexpectedness of the action, and an intuitive feeling that she was about to be kissed, made Cara's pulse race, and she could feel her heart begin to thud against her ribs. She could not recall any moment in her past when she had wanted—or imagined—Martin Dante to kiss her, but she could not conjure up a single reason to stop him now that the event seemed imminent.

His chiseled features were intense as he slid his hands to her back, pulling her to him. Neither of them said a word, at least not a word that could have been recorded on a tape. His eyes were saying something elemental, flashing the message that their coming together was as unavoidable as breathing, and could be

put off no longer. They sparkled with his urgent need
to know the feel of her lips, the taste of her mouth.

She swallowed spasmodically as she absorbed his
message, her lips opening very slightly in unconscious
invitation. Were her tattletale eyes telling him that it
was all right? Why they would was a total mystery to
her!

He bent to tease her lips, as though he were testing
to see if they were too hot to touch. The tiny impact
tilted Cara's head up. He saw her small surrender, and
pulled her body closer to his as he again lowered his
mouth to hers. This time his lips held hers with a ten-
derness that surprised her. The intimacy was so soft
that she could not deny it. Relaxing within his arms,
she delighted in the gentle nipping of his teeth as they
pulled at her lower lip. The tingle that the tiny bites
generated danced along her nerve endings, igniting
long-dormant feelings inside her.

With a sigh, she lifted her arms to his neck, pulling
her taut breasts into the crispness of his shirt. The
waistband of her sweat top was breached, as he moved
his hand to her bare back. How warm it felt against
her cool skin. She wasn't happy that her body wanted
his hand there. Neither was she pleased that her mouth
was equally eager to invite his tongue inside. He accepted her invitation, and his questing tongue slid between her teeth. Again, she heard herself sigh, feeling
an unnatural helplessness against the emotional on-
slaught of his kisses and the awakening of her long-
sleeping need. Her body trembled. What could mere
flesh-and-bones determination do in the face of such

a strong, lusty hunger—especially when the hunger was being eased by this heady, delectable meal.

Martin groaned against her lips as she became the wanton hostess to his exploration of the recesses of her mouth. She could feel his appetite for her heighten in the delicious throbbing of his loins.

She was hot, damp, her mind swirling in a crimson storm of desire for this completely inappropriate man. How could this happen? She thought she had insulated herself from this kind of madness long ago. Men were too much the takers to invest such eager emotions in.

She had taught herself to cut them off with a word, a look or—a defiant toss of the head. And here she was, on the brink of clawing this wealthy conservative snob right out of his clothes!

She groaned as his kisses moved down beyond her jaw to the sensitive skin behind her ear. Some vague sort of negative cry gurgled in her throat as the dregs of her determination worked desperately to stop this insanity before it was too late. But even in her own ears the solitary wail of denial sounded like an impassioned cry of need.

The hand beneath her shirt moved to cup a breast. His thumb, with its electrifying flicking of the swollen tip, began the short remaining distance toward driving her mad.

He lifted her shirt and lowered himself to his knees. Her legs felt weak, and she leaned a shoulder against the refrigerator for support. The metal surface felt cold against her fiery skin.

His tongue replaced his thumb, and he pulled her breasts to him, breathing in the sweetness of her body, and kneading the tempting flesh between his hands. Hands of an artist, so sensitive, so—

What the hell was she doing! She knew she was drowning, going down for the third time. It was now or never! Her mind screamed the question that had to be answered. What the hell was she letting Martin Dante do? She didn't even like this man, and here he was, kissing her breasts as if he had a right to!

With trembling hands that wanted only to enfold his head between aching fingers and pull him closer, she pushed hard against his broad shoulders. "Martin!" It was a ragged exhalation. "Good Lord! Stop this—now!"

At the sound of her throaty demand, he lifted his head, raising those glorious bedroom eyes to meet hers. His expression was exceedingly soft. The sight was beautiful—this man, this polished gentleman, unmasked by passion. It would have made her happy to know she had the power to scratch that polish, even this little bit, except for the fact he had also managed to breach her spiky little barriers, a feat no man in a very long time could boast.

His hands still encircled her rib cage in a halo of warmth. It was hard to get her legs to move away from him, but move she did, sweeping his arms from her as she retreated. Trying for a sophisticated nonchalance, she forced a laugh. It sounded false, even in her ears. "Well . . . Martin. That was certainly refreshing." She crossed her arms protectively about her. "Next time, though, I think I'll take the Gatorade." She was still smiling. She hoped. She didn't care for him to get a hint of the truth about how his kisses had totally disarmed her. How they'd made her forget her distaste of men in general, and him in particular.

He moved slowly to stand before her. For a silent moment, he watched her, his lids lowered, long lashes hiding his eyes. They were standing only inches apart, and she could smell the pleasant woodsy scent of his cologne. The air between them was charged, and her spine tingled with an odd combination of excitement and fear at his close, quiet perusal. She would have taken another step away, but found herself imprisoned against the kitchen's center island.

The urge to break and run became very strong, but the old Torrence pride was even stronger. So, instead, she lifted a regal chin. "I think I'll get those charts and go, Martin. We've taken up enough of each other's time."

He pursed his lips, and then with a rueful half smile, he shook his head. "Will you accept my apology first? I don't usually accost women in my kitchen."

It was defensive, and childish, she knew, but she couldn't keep herself from challenging, "Oh, no? Where do you usually accost them?"

There was a note of surprise in his chuckle as he took her arm, leading her toward the living room. "You never let a man get the last word, do you?"

"Not anymore." She lifted her arm from his. "Now, if you'll give me your pants, I'll be going."

His deep laughter caught her off guard. Why was he in such a damned good mood when she felt so rotten?

Chapter Five

Martin quickened his pace as he headed toward the University of Tulsa library. He shook his head at his lapse of sanity, squinting against the sun as it reflected off the tall, stained-glass windows of Sharp Chapel. Here he was, between meetings, trudging around a college campus after a woman whom he had no business associating with. Her connections with Raleigh Younger and Donnelly Wakefield made seeing her a valid problem. Not to mention the fact that she wanted to associate with him the way she wanted a wart on her nose.

He checked his watch. The sociology department secretary had said Cara was having a lunch seminar with a group of students on the plaza between the library and the chapel. When he lost the shaded protection of the Westby Center walkway, the hot July wind tugged at his suit coat, and a scorching sun blazed down on his head. He shrugged out of the coat. Why he wondered, was he out here in ninety-degree heat when he could be eating lunch at the plush Tulsa Club as he usually did on Wednesday afternoons?

Nothing about this made any sense. But after yesterday in his kitchen he couldn't make himself stay away. He'd kissed her. He hadn't meant to, it had just happened. And when it did, he discovered something intriguing about the curly-headed hand grenade that even thinking about made his loins ache.

Cara Torrence was one hell of a woman under all that armor. He wondered what had happened to her to make her so protective of herself that she had to keep people—no, correct that—men, a spear's length away? But yesterday, probably as much to her surprise as his, she'd shed her armor for just a moment. And it had been long enough. He'd seen the desirable woman that she was, and it was too tempting a discovery to walk away from. No matter how sensible an idea that might be.

"To hell with politics and to hell with logic," he mumbled. He was going to see Cara and he was going to ask her out, and if anyone questioned his business ethics, he'd tell them to go to hell.

He rounded a corner of the library and paused beneath the stingy shade of a stunted ornamental tree and scanned the plaza. She was there. There could be no mistaking the group of young people lounging along the edge of a large planter or cross-legged on the cement in the shade of a spreading oak.

Cara was standing, addressing the group. He could hear the clear feline purr of her laughter as she gestured in that exaggerated, but graceful way that was so unique. There was a titter of laughter and Martin grinned, picturing the wild-eyed, radical sociologists she would be turning out to terrorize the public in a few years.

She put her hands on her hips and cocked her head as one of the students began to talk. He was fascinated by the curve of her hips beneath the white cotton slacks. The blouse she wore was white, too, with ruffles dancing about the wide neck. He noticed with amusement that the loose blouse dropped off of one shoulder. Atypical clothing for a professor, but typical of Professor Torrence, he surmised.

Movement out of the corner of his eye caught his attention. Cara and her students were fifty feet ahead of him. And some twenty feet from them on Martin's right, a husky man was hurrying stealthily in their direction. Martin came to a dead stop as the man paused, half crouched behind a crape myrtle. Something small and steely glistened in one hand.

Now the man was about ten feet from the group. With shocking suddenness, he began to run, pushing through the unsuspecting students who were sitting on the paved plaza, knocking several to the ground.

He reached Cara and lifted his hand toward her. Martin's jaw clenched in horror as he realized that the thing in his fist was a gun.

A deafening crack split the air. As Martin began to run, he heard a shrill scream and watched helplessly as Cara crumpled to the ground.

"What the hell?" he growled, unable to believe his eyes.

The man had taken off in the direction Martin was charging. Martin shouted, "What have you done, you filthy bastard!" His fist rammed into the gunman's face, dropping him like a fly on a swatter. His chubby features registered surprise, and he lost consciousness and sank with a dull thud facedown on the ground.

Martin frowned, confused, at the clean-cut youthfulness of the attacker. He bent down to get a closer look. The unconscious man couldn't have been more than nineteen years old.

"Martin! What are you doing here? What have you done to Dennis?"

He looked up from his squat over the prostrate young man. Cara was standing there looking down at them both, her expression, flushed and windswept, no less shocked than his.

"Cara! What in God's name? I thought he'd shot you!"

The sound of running feet caught their attention, and Martin looked beyond her to see the students on their way to join them. Cara spun around and held up both her hands. "No! No! Go back. You'll spoil everything if you come over here." They came to a skidding halt as she waved them away. "Now just go back and sit under the tree. I'll be right there." Dropping to her knees, she confronted Martin with a whispered cry. "Is this what the rich do when they go slumming—beat up people?"

"Cara!" Martin tried to ignore the fact that she was berating him for bringing down her assailant, but he couldn't hide the serrated edge of his words. "I thought this—this person just shot you! What did you expect me to do, loan him a couple of bucks for a get-away cab? What the hell is going on here?" His mercury-colored eyes glittered with frustration.

"Oh, Martin." She heaved an exasperated sigh. "Well, for one thing, you just decked the assistant football coach's nephew."

His brow lifted in surprise. "What the— Damn it, woman, I've never hit a man before, let alone a kid!"

Pushing her hair back out of her face, she ignored his frustrated outburst and bent to examine the youth's injury. She softly stroked his head. "Dennis? Dennis, are you okay?"

He moaned, lifting his head slightly and shaking it. Martin could hear him spit dirt, and winced. "Cara, I thought—" He took her wrist. "He did have a gun, didn't he? Where is it?"

Very shakily, Dennis raised up on one elbow. His upper lip was swelling and turning blue. Cara sucked in a breath, putting a hand on his cheek. "Oh, Dennis, I'm sorry." She touched Martin's arm. "This man is a friend of mine." She turned to eye him narrowly and slapped his arm with the back of her hand. "He wants to apologize to you. Don't you, Martin?"

"I want an explanation," he gritted.

She reached behind her and picked something up. "Here's the gun. Now apologize to Dennis."

"If you say so." He lifted a skeptical brow, eyeing her profile as she ran a soothing hand through the young man's hair. He felt a twinge of discomfort as he watched her hands move gently along the younger man's temple. Between clenched jaws, he growled, "Sorry, kid. Want me to call you a cab?"

Cara gasped, straightening. She flung a bare shoulder around so that she could better face him. "Martin, how can you joke at a time like this?"

"At a time like what? I don't know what's going on."

"For your information, this was supposed to be an experiment—memory under stress." She lifted a challenging brow as if to dare him to find fault. When he said nothing, she added no less stiffly, "I didn't originate the exercise, it's done at a lot of universities. The gun was filled with blanks. If you insist, I'll explain later. But right now we have to take care of Dennis."

Martin stared at her for a long moment. "Hell," he mumbled under his breath, "I should have known it'd be something like that." Releasing her arm, he directed his attention to the boy on the ground. "I'm sorry, Dennis. Can you sit up?" When Dennis nodded, Martin helped him to a sitting position. "How do you feel?"

"Like—cwap."

"Hell!" Martin repeated the curse, muttering it between clenched jaws.

"Yeah. Dat, too." Dennis squinted up at Martin. "Got a had-ka-chief, Wocky?" His swollen lip distorted his words.

"Sure, kid." He pulled one from his hip pocket and handed it to him. "I'm sorry. I thought you'd shot Cara." He turned his narrowed look toward her.

"Why I jumped to that conclusion is anybody's guess."

Sitting back on the grass, Cara acted as though she hadn't heard Martin's sardonic remark. She critically examined Dennis's face, trying to put Martin out of her thoughts. With one last pat on Dennis's shoulder, she suggested solemnly, "I think we'd better get you into a cool place. You're a little pale. And I need to get back to the students and see if I can salvage the project." She took Dennis's hand in both of hers. "I'm going to have Martin take you to my office." She turned toward Martin and gave him her most disapproving look. "Mr. Dante will have one of the nurses come to look at you. Then, if your teeth feel solid enough, he'll be glad to get you anything you want for lunch. Isn't that right, Martin?"

"Absolutely." Martin's smile was apologetic as he put a supporting hand under the boy's shoulder.

Dennis nodded. "I . . ." He sniffed, wiping at his nose. "Tanks."

"Oh, it's the least he can do." Cara patted Dennis's hand. "By the way, you were wonderful." She stood, brushing the dry grass from her pants. With a petulant pout, she eyed Martin directly. "As for you, take good care of Dennis. He knows where my office is. I'll be there in about fifteen minutes."

Cara breezed into her office, coming to a halt when she saw that Martin was alone. "Where's Dennis?"

"I took him to the University health centre." He grimaced and flexed his feet. "He's going to be fine, but they have to make sure his nose isn't broken."

Cara lifted her eyes toward the ceiling. "Lord."

Martin stood up and came over to her. "I'm taking care of everything. But . . ." He hesitated.

When her eyes met his, he was very close. "I am not going to apologize to you about this. I thought you'd been hurt and I acted instinctively." His face was set, daring her to argue.

She didn't. Even feeling the way she did about him, her lips twitched with begrudging humor at the vision of him slugging someone in her defense. Very reluctantly, she admitted, "I won't ask you to apologize to me, Martin. I guess I'd have to expect a man like you to rush into the fray, considering your chivalrous upbringing and all. At least you're no coward."

"You make chivalry sound like a crime."

"Do I?" She was flip and offhand about it, trying hard not to be touched by his attempt to save her. "Besides," she said shrugging, "the project appears to be salvaged. I left a graduate assistant with the students to take eyewitness reports." She pushed a drooping ruffle up to cover a bare shoulder. "So far, Dennis has been described as 150 to 210 pounds, and between eighteen and thirty-two years of age." She couldn't restrain a short laugh. "Stress can really mess up the mind."

"I'm beginning to find that out." There was a tinge of humour in his voice. "By the way, thanks for the compliment."

"What compliment?" She retorted defensively.

"You said I wasn't a coward." He put his index finger beneath her chin and tilted her face upward. "Thanks for that, anyway."

"Uh—oh." She backed away, suddenly very aware of the magnificent spread of his shoulders and the subtle scent of him in the tiny office. Annoyed with herself, she turned quickly away and began to aimlessly shuffle the clutter on her desk. "What are you doing on campus anyway, Martin?" She didn't try to hide the irritation she felt. "If you want your pants back, they won't be ready until after four." She pretended to be organizing a stack of papers. "I figured you had plenty of pants, so I decided not to pay extra for the one-hour cleaning job."

"Cara, I told you yesterday, I don't care about the damn pants. Insisting on having them cleaned was your idea."

She stopped stacking papers. His voice seemed vaguely tense now. Good. Her lips lifted slightly as she asked, "Then why are you here?"

"To ask you to lunch."

"Lunch?" The smile faded. "Why me?"

"Why not?" His voice was sharper. Was it frustration, anger or shock at her hesitation to leap at his invitation? She took a deep breath and declined. "I don't think so, Martin. A glass of water with you is about all I can han—stand."

He didn't reply, and her curiosity about how he took her rejection began to eat away at her resolve not to turn around. Refusals being few and far between for him, he was probably glowering at her, or at the very least, standing there slack-jawed, in disbelief.

She couldn't bear the suspense. When she turned, she was surprised to see that he was smiling. A treacherous thrill rushed through her at the sight of the slashing dimple that had appeared in his right cheek.

He lifted his jacket from the back of the chair and began to shrug it on. "I think you'll like the Duke of Kensington. Great English food, and it has a dart board. I bet you love darts." He looked down at his watch, adding, "It's nearly one o'clock. We'd better go. I have a meeting at three with..." He let the sentence die away, and his brows converged to resemble a hawk diving for prey.

She let the "darts" remark go, asking sarcastically, "With whom? Or can't you remember?"

He lifted his sleepy gaze to her face, his smile skeptical. "No. I just forgot for a minute to whom I was speaking."

"Smooth talker. No woman can resist a man who can't remember who she is." Leaning back against her desk, she asked, astonished at her interest, "So who is this mystery meeting with that I can't know about? Another woman?"

He grinned that dazzling grin again. "No. Mathison. He and some of his people are coming up from Oklahoma City to meet with me in my condo."

Cara stiffened. "Mathison!" She crossed her arms before her, presenting him with a stern stare. "You're going to consort with the enemy in your very home? Right under my nose?"

A devilish light kindled in his silvery eyes. "I'm afraid so. But not quite so pleasantly as I did with you yesterday, I dare say."

Her cheeks grew hot at the seductiveness of that twinkle, and she tried to force the memory from her mind. Pouncing on a subject that was far from safe, but certainly safer than this one, she probed. "About that, Martin. I mean—your helping with the Mathison campaign. I understand your job requires it. But you must have a favorite candidate. It is Donnelly Wakefield, isn't it? You can tell me."

"I'll tell you one thing. I'm out of my mind to be seen with you." He took her hand and shook his head in a gesture of self-deprecation. "Let's go to lunch."

"Oh, sure." She tried to pull away. "With a charming invitation like that, I'd be an idiot to refuse."

He held her fast, leading her toward the office door. "Don't get huffy on me, Cara. I meant, I don't—can't have a favorite candidate. And my association with you could be considered a conflict of interest."

"Association? We have no association, Martin." This time, she managed to pull out of his grasp, halting at the door. "Maybe we'd better forget the lunch. I'd hate for you to lose your perch on the fence because of an alleged association with me—however ridiculous the notion!"

"Take it easy, Cara. I was trying to compliment you." He took her by her elbow and headed down the hall, grumbling, "I swear to heaven, you and I are going to have lunch today if it kills us both."

"This is kidnapping, you know," she snapped, as he pulled her down the corridor.

"Go ahead and scream. People will just think it's another one of your stress projects." Martin reached out to open the door for her.

By force of habit, she beat him to it, pushing it open for them both. "Why must you pick on me?"

His grin was crooked. "Damned if I know." Lightly, he put his hand to the small of her back, turning her in the direction of the parking lot.

Bright sunlight made her squint, disguising her disturbed frown. Why was she allowing him to maneuver her this way? She didn't want to go to lunch with him. She didn't want to be with him at all! So why in heaven's name was she going?

Chapter Six

Cara didn't want to dwell on why she was still with Martin Dante when they reached the Kensington Galleria. Somehow his determination to have lunch with her had won out over her determination not to. So now there was little to do but get through it. She'd never been to the Duke of Kensington before and felt a little underdressed when they walked into the plush pub. "Lord, Martin—" she made one last ditch plea for escape "—I'm not dressed for this place." The costumed girl at the reservations desk lifted her eyes to them and smiled.

Martin smiled back, and said quietly to her, "No problem. We can get in."

She grimaced. "That's not what I meant."

The young woman moved to meet them. "Good afternoon, Mr. Dante. Will there be two for lunch?"

"Yes, Molly." Martin took Cara's arm. "And we don't have much time. I think we'll have the charbroiled halibut with lemon butter sauce."

The woman nodded, leading them up a short flight of carpeted steps. The room was long, full of polished mahogany tables and rust-red velvet chairs. Brass light fixtures and hanging planters shone in golden contrast to the dark, rich furnishings. Cara glanced over a brass railing on their right. A level two feet lower than the restaurant held a thirty-foot-long bar. The place exuded old-world charm, she had to admit, even in her distress.

Cara became more uncomfortable when they passed two perfectly acceptable, empty tables. She cast a questioning glance toward Martin. "Where is she taking us, to the commoners' section?"

Martin grinned, but didn't answer. Just then the waitress stopped, turned and motioned them into a small room that held one rather narrow table and four chairs, two on each side. "Here you are, sir, ma'am."

Cara peered inside. "Here?"

With a hand at her waist, Martin coaxed her into the room. "Here."

Once Cara had been seated, the waitress asked, "Would you care for a drink, ma'am?"

She thought she should probably say no, but she felt in need of one. "Sure. What do you recommend?"

"We have regular mixed drinks as well as English beers—served both warm and cold."

"Oh?" Inspiration clutched her by the throat, and she smiled. "Well, then, I'll have your best English beer—warm, by all means."

Martin coughed.

"And the usual for you, Mr. Dante?"

He nodded and the waitress was gone. As he seated himself beside Cara at the table, she scanned the small room. It was lavishly decorated. The ceiling was made of tin, painted and embossed with an intricate design; the walls were papered in off-white with a royal crest design in rust-red velvet. Candles glittered on the table, because the room was dark for midday. She swallowed uneasily. She could feel Martin's warmth, and her body was reacting to it with an increased pulse rate. She didn't like the fact that she was unable to feel indifferent toward this man.

When he moved to lay a casual arm behind her chair, she reacted protectively, shoving it away with an elbow. Pretending to plant her elbow casually on the chair back, she swiveled toward him. "Uh...you must come here often," she blurted with false casualness.

He sat back. "Yes. I'm one of the owners."

Her lips parted in surprise. "Owner—you're kidding."

He shrugged. "No. The idea intrigued me, so I bought in. That mahogany bar and all these tables were shipped from England. It's the most authentic English pub in the United States."

She removed her elbow from the chair back and folded her arms. "So, that's why you have your own dining room."

"It's not mine. If it's empty, anybody can request it."

She sniffed derisively. "How democratic."

He chuckled as the waitress brought their drinks. When she had gone, Cara eyed her beer critically and then his glass. "What are you having?"

His lips twitched with barely veiled humor. "Water." She knew what he was thinking—recalling. Hastily she took a sip of her beer. It was bitter. Closing one eye, she swallowed with difficulty. "Ugh." She wiped foam off her upper lip with a napkin. "That's terrible stuff."

He lifted his glass toward her. "Have some of mine?" This time he allowed himself to smile directly at her, his drowsy eyes glistening with fun.

"Never mind." She pushed the water away. "I'll get used to this."

He took a sip before he put his glass down. "You'll like the halibut."

She countered, "What if I don't? What if halibut makes me swell up and turn green? You could have asked me."

He sat forward, lacing his fingers together on the tabletop. His smile grew crooked. "You'll like it."

He was so used to getting his way he didn't even consider alternatives! In order to keep from spewing out her opinion regarding his insensitivity, she lifted her mug to thinned lips and took a big swallow. Closing her eyes, she forced the drink down. How did the English drink this stuff—especially on a hot summer day?

"Used to it yet?" Martin asked casually.

"I will. I will. Just drink your water." She pushed her hair away from her neck. It was getting warm.

"What did you say you have to do this afternoon?"

She shifted in her chair to better see him. "I don't have anything until six, when I teach aerobics."

"Oh? Tell me about that." He shifted, too. When his knee touched hers, she moved away.

"Haven't you ever watched us? Most men do, who are up there jogging on the track."

He shook his head. "I don't usually jog that late. What have I been missing?"

She put an elbow on the table. "From *your* viewpoint, I guess I'd have to say 'jiggling.'"

"Jiggling?" he repeated with a lift of one brow. "Sounds interesting. Maybe I'll drop by sometime."

She turned away and took a sip of her beer. It tasted better, so she took a long draw. "Sure, why not?" She put the glass down with a thud. "Bring Mathison. Might need to know about other career opportunities, come November. He's already pretty good with the old fast shuffle. I might let him substitute-teach for me."

The halibut arrived, and Cara had to admit, if only to herself, that it was delicious. As she downed the remainder of her mug of beer, Martin offered, "Do you ever jog?"

She blinked up at him. "What?"

"Do you jog?"

She shook her head. "No. Too monotonous."

"But jogging is better exercise than the dancing you girls do. Jiggling can't be strenuous enough to be very aerobic."

She choked on a piece of broccoli. If she'd been able to speak she would have told him to go straight to hell. How dare he suggest that what she did was less important or less beneficial. Just because rhythmic aerobics was an exercise method mostly chosen by females didn't mean it was a stepsister to "real" exercise! She was unable to speak for long enough to cool down a bit. She supposed that, being a man, Martin would believe what he wanted to believe. Why give herself indigestion over it? Wiping watering eyes with her napkin, she decided brevity would be the wisest course, croaking, "No—actually, no."

"Are you all right? Would you like some water?"

She looked up at him, barely suppressed violence shimmering in her eyes. "I'd rather have another beer."

Fifteen minutes later, the halibut gone, she put down her second empty mug of beer. "That's pretty good," she admitted with a tilt of her head. This time her smile wasn't forced. "Warm beer grows on you, I guess." She shook her head, lifting her hair off her shoulders again. "Whew. It's hot in here, don't you think?"

He seemed surprised. "No."

She screwed up her face. "No? Boy, I'm hot."

He smiled knowingly. "Maybe it's the warm beer."

She squinted up at him, her eyes focusing sluggishly. "Two beers?" Waving the idea away with a flourish, she knocked his water glass over. Ice clattered along the table and into his lap.

Her eyes followed the slithery trail the cubes left on the table until it disappeared over the edge. "Oh! Damn!" She dived automatically to retrieve the ice.

He moved quickly, too, taking her wrist firmly. "Don't help me, Cara." With a brisk sweep, he brushed the ice to the floor.

"I never spill things." Distress edged her words. "Honestly. I never do. I can't believe this."

He squeezed her wrist reassuringly. "Forget it."

She averted her gaze, troubled that this man seemed to turn her into a dimwit with ten thumbs every time they were together. "I feel terrible about this." Her face was flushed, she knew.

His hand slid to hers. "Cara. It was just a little ice."

She didn't pull her hand away, and wasn't quite sure why. But to soothe her pride, she turned to look at him again. "Well, nevertheless, I'm buying the lunch. Remember, there's still the matter of the coat I ruined."

He shook his head. "You're not paying for lunch. Don't be ridiculous."

She bristled. Ridiculous, was she? Through tightened lips, she repeated, "My treat, Martin. Let's not argue."

He lifted a brow. "You get generous when you're tipsy, I see. That's good to know."

Her eyes widened. "Tipsy! I've never been tipsy a day in my life!"

His lips lifted in a grin. "Have you ever been generous a day in your life?"

She frowned. "What is that supposed to mean?"

He lifted a hand to her hair, rubbing a curl between two fingers. "I mean the lunch is paid for. Remember, I own the place. So if you insist on making some sort of payment, I'll accept a kiss and call it even—suit coat, lunch and all."

She stood abruptly. It proved to be a stupid idea. The quick movement made her dizzy. She reached out for support to keep from falling, and made a grab for his shoulders.

He caught her waist, pulling her into his lap. "Cara..." His lips were seductively soft against her ear. He drew her to him, so close she could feel the heavy beating of his heart against her chest.

She lifted her chin so that she could meet his gaze. "What?" she asked, feeling woozy, befuddled.

"Drop your guard..." he murmured against her mouth, taking possession of her parted lips.

He moved a hand to the back of her head, deepening the kiss. Cara blinked, wide-eyed with surprise, a little too slow in her mental processes. By the time she knew what was happening, she was being kissed too well to pull away. A caressing hand moved up from her waist to cup a breast, and she moaned against his mouth. But to her shock, she was moaning with desire.

Her eyelids lolled closed, and caught in the hypnotic spell of his taste and scent, she lifted her arms to encircle his neck. Her fingers delighted in the feel of his soft, fine hair.

He lifted his lips from hers with a reluctant sigh. "Tonight—" he kissed the corner of her mouth, and then the tip of her nose "—I'll be by about eight-thirty to pick up those pants. You will be home, won't you?"

Her eyes were still closed as she nodded.

"Good," he murmured huskily, smoothing her hair away from her face. When she opened her eyes, he lifted his lips in a crooked smile. "We'd better go."

She swallowed, feeling a rush of embarrassment as rationality returned and she got a full mental picture of what had just happened. And what was worse, she could feel, from her position on his lap, that he was highly aroused. Much to her amazement, so was she. Angry at her insane weakness where this man was concerned, she clamped his shoulders with stiff fingers and pushed herself up onto unsteady legs. "Yes. Besides, you have a hard—er, a difficult meeting..." She felt herself go crimson, and didn't meet his eyes.

"About tonight—" he took her arm "—I'll pick up steaks or something. We could make dinner."

"No. Forget it." She was definite. "I don't cook." Everything looked blurry as he led her back toward the entrance. But it didn't matter much. Nothing mattered except the painful throbbing in her core. It would be stupid, only ending up causing her pain, if she let this go further. "I don't think it would be a good idea, Martin."

The young woman standing at the reservation desk nodded a smile toward them as Martin handed her several bills. "Thanks, Molly." He put a casual arm about Cara's shoulder as he bid the smiling woman goodbye.

"Goodbye, Mr. Dante," the attractive woman purred. "Come again, soon."

Even in Cara's agitated state, she could hear the wistful sound in the young woman's words, and gritted her teeth. She was sure Martin Dante was an ex-

pert at making a woman his babbling slave. She would
have to avoid him at all costs.

"What are you afraid of, Cara?"

"What?" She jerked to look up at him. "Afraid?"

His look was enigmatic. "Is it me?"

She refused to be intimidated—even by the truth.
"I'm not afraid of you. That's idiotic."

"Good," he noted with a grin. "Then I'll see you
at eight-thirty for dinner."

"I...uh..." Caught off guard, she favored him with
a grim frown, feeling manipulated. The smooth con-
niver had left her but two choices. She could either
admit that she was afraid to be alone with him, or she
could shore up her defenses and suffer through the
evening. But, she swore, if she had to suffer, so would
he! She'd teach him to manipulate her! Turning away,
she acquiesced begrudgingly. "All right. Eight-thirty.
But if there's going to be any dinner, you're going to
do the cooking."

Eight twenty-eight. Cara looked at her watch for the
tenth time in the ten minutes since she'd heard Martin's car rumble into his parking space. Standing at the
mirror in her sparsely furnished bedroom, she examined her hair. It stood out in all directions. She ran her
fingers up and forward through it, ruffing it further.
Pursing her lips, she turned her head slowly from side
to side to watch her face catch the light. The heavy
moisturizer she'd applied had left an unappetizing
sheen to her face. Good. If this unruly creature didn't
turn him off, nothing would.

She unfastened the top button of her huge fatigue shirt spreading out the V to expose a hint of chest. She frowned. "What are you doing, Cara!" Quickly, and with an irritated flick of her finger, she did it up again.

She smoothed the rough shirt over baggy fatigue pants. Both top and pants were clean, but paint-spattered. Her smile was a satisfied smirk. "Turn-off city," she mumbled as the doorbell chimed. Martin was here. She wrinkled her nose at herself, and marched determinedly out of the room. She was sure, once he saw her, he wouldn't be there long.

She pulled the door wide. "Hello..." Her words died on her lips as she saw a pair of heavily loaded arms, and the top of a dark head.

"Hi. I hope you're hungry."

He couldn't see her! Cara winced, reluctantly reaching for the middle bag. How could she turn him off if he couldn't see her? "Here, let me have one of those."

Without protest, Martin let her take one of the three bags out of his arms. "Thanks. I got a little carried away—I thought you might enjoy making Pavlova for dessert. Takes a lot of stuff."

"Me?" She stepped back, shifting the bag to one hip so that he could get most of the effect of her face and outfit. "I don't even enjoy dumping soup out of a can."

He shifted his bags and stepped inside before he looked directly at her. His grin faded into an expression close to shock as he took in her baggy, spattered clothes, and her shiny face and frizzy hair.

"Well?" she coaxed after a moment of silence. "What's wrong?"

"Nothing. I just didn't expect..." His mouth quirked up at one corner. "Does this one have a name?"

"A name?"

He cocked his head. "Your clown outfit. Who are you supposed to be, Sergeant Bela Lugosi?"

"I beg your pardon?" Her eyes became hazel slits, but secretly, she was loving his puzzled expression. "I'm just dressed casually. If my attire offends you, you don't have to stay."

"This is what you call casual?" His eyes flicked from her head to her feet and back again before he added, "Do you dress for battle whenever you entertain men in your home?"

She blanched, retorting defensively, "Don't be stupid."

"I'll try not to be." He tried again. "Did you just wash your hair?"

As he strolled toward her, she unwilling inspected his slender height. "No. I just thought I'd try something different." He was too near. She fought the need to back away, asking defiantly, "You like it?"

He grunted and shook his head. "Cara." His gaze was penetrating. "Why do I get the feeling you're afraid of being imprisoned in a kitchen, and you're doing everything in your power to get me to leave."

"Will you get off it, Martin?" She tried to ignore the silvery devilment in his eyes. Pivoting toward the kitchen, she argued, "I am not afraid, for Pete's sake!"

"A kitchen isn't a prison, Cara. What happened? You get locked in a greasy spoon as a child?"

"Funny man." She shot him a glare and turned away to begin emptying her sack.

He put his groceries down beside hers. Shrugging off his gray suit coat, he murmured, "Maybe a greasy man?"

She winced. Pretending she hadn't heard him, she motioned absently toward the living room. "Ice and everything is in there. If you insist on going through with this meal thing, you can start by fixing me a glass of white wine while I sort through this stuff."

"One white wine, coming up."

Reluctantly, she began unloading the other two sacks, covertly watching him leave the kitchen with his lithe, masculine gracefulness. Absentmindedly, she lifted a plastic bag of mushrooms from a sack, wondering if Martin would be surprised to know that she had not entertained a man alone in her condominium since she'd moved in over two years ago—and for a year before that in her last apartment.

"Would you like it in here or in there?" he called.

"In there!" Quickly she disposed of the things that needed refrigeration, and then, with one more steadying breath, she hurried into her living room.

"Thanks, Jeeves." She didn't smile as she took the stemmed glass from his fingers.

"You're welcome, soldier." He poured some soda into his glass. "Would you mind if I sat down?"

He had a drink in his hand, and he wanted to sit down. Apparently her ploy to get him to leave hadn't worked. With a small sigh, she motioned carelessly toward the couch. "I suppose not."

"Thanks." As he settled down, he studied her. "You have a nice place, Cara."

Not wanting to be too near, she perched on one worn arm of the couch. "It is nice," she agreed. No power on earth would have gotten her to admit to Martin Dante that her furniture was tired and old, and no amount of polite flattery would change that. Taking a sip of her wine, she remarked as casually as she could, "I'm buying things as I can." She pointed to an antique apothecary chest standing along the dining-area wall. Her one fine piece. A brass wall sconce was hung near one end, and at the other was an array of candlesticks holding candles of different heights. "That came from an estate sale. I'm proud of that little find."

"Mother would kill for that piece."

Cara laughed derisively. Placing her glass on a wicker end table that was actually a basket turned upside down, she said, "Don't patronize me, Martin. Isobel Dante probably has twelve of those in her basement." Resting a hand behind her on the arm of the couch, she fingered a loose thread. He was making her nervous with his nearness, and she wanted to get this over! "Well, don't you think you'd better get the food started?"

He reached across her lap, grazing her legs as he put his glass beside hers. "You're the boss."

Her legs registered his touch with singular importance. Suddenly she had an insane urge to be swept into his arms again. Fighting the feeling, she abruptly stood. "Right. I'm the boss."

She had taken only one step toward the kitchen, when he circled her wrist with his fingers. "You try to be so damned tough—" he stood, moving to face her "—and to look so damned ridiculous." The hand at her wrist moved to her back. With a husky note in his voice, he asked, "Why is that, Cara?" Silver eyes shining, he pulled her to him. She could neither speak nor resist as he held her in the encompassing energy of his arms.

His breath feathered her lips, tantalizing them as he coaxed softly, "don't be afraid to let a man get close."

"No...I—" Her voice broke. Frightened now of herself and her weakness for him, she arched away, pressing her hands against his chest, pleading, "Martin—just take your pants and leave."

"Later..." he muttered, his hard male lips trailing along her cheek. Her heart hammered with a heady mixture of fear and anticipation of his kiss. Her body was pulsating from icy cold to fiery hot, short-circuiting, going haywire within his embrace. When those warm, persuasive lips melted into hers, she could do no more than lean helplessly into his long, hard length.

She felt herself being lifted into his arms, but she didn't even try to resist him. Unable to fathom the reasons, she was aching for this man. She hadn't wanted a man this badly in a long time. If the truth be known, she hadn't wanted a man at all in a long time! And here she was allowing herself to be carried to bed like some mindless fool.

But that was just the trouble. She was mindless—at the moment she was completely without reason— nothing further up than her throbbing lips was functioning properly—and she wasn't even too sure about her lips. She felt so dizzy and breathless that she could do no more than cling to Martin and lay her head against his starched collar.

He smelled awfully good, and she inhaled deeply. It wasn't one of those familiar scents that she could recognize from any men's department counter. But it was clean, warm and potent.

She felt the softness of her chenille spread come up to meet her. At the same time, Martin's arms loosened their hold, and his hands journeyed caressingly around her body, moving up to cup her face. His lips came down again to taste hers, and his tongue, like an artist's brush, outlined her lips as he ran his fingers through her hair.

He kissed the tip of her nose as he put his hands to her waist and lifted her up to lean against a row of throw pillows cushioning the headboard. When she looked into his eyes, she was awed by their clear beauty. His soft smile was wonderful to behold, so full of promise.

He was leaning over her, exuding whatever it was that was making her fall headlong off her "to hell with Martin Dante soapbox;" his eyes were so drowsily aware of her that she couldn't keep her hands off him. Reaching up, she began to loosen his tie, whispering, "Did you know, you have bedroom eyes?"

"Do I?" he murmured.

He watched her—just watched her as she began to unbutton his shirt. "My mother would say so," she answered as she finished, lowering lashes, and feeling strangely shy.

He pulled his shirt from his belted trousers, shaking his head as he remarked quietly, "I've never known what that was supposed to mean..." Taking her hands in his, he kissed each palm in its turn, muttering against the sensitive skin, "Touch me, Cara."

She thrilled at the unexpected catch in his voice. It seemed as though he dared not hope that she was really giving herself to him. Little did he know that to get her this far had been a hurdle so strewn with thorny words and the debris of other suitors, it was nearly impassable. But it was a hurdle Martin had already conquered. Her smile was melancholy as she slipped her hands inside his opened shirt to explore the muscular breadth of his chest. The taut flesh was hard and strong beneath the wiry mat of dark hair. The highly male feel of him was all it took. Pent-up desires she had kept chained and under control for too long exploded. She curled her arms about his back. Pulling him to her with all of her womanly strength, she teased his nipples with her tongue, sighing his name.

The thudding of his heart and his deep moan of pleasure tickled her lips as she unfastened his belt. He turned slightly on his side so that she could more easily unclasp his trousers. Lifting his tensed, lean hips, he helped as she slid the pants down over them.

"God," he croaked against her ear as he reached down and took her hand. Lifting her palm to his lips he kissed it, again. Very deliberately he unfastened every button on her coarse shirt before sliding it tenderly over her shoulders and off her arms. He sat up and removed her sandals before he helped her slip the slacks over her hips and down her legs. Before removing her lacy panties, he curved his fingers beneath the band of one leg, exploring the softness there.

He stroked her, very leisurely, and each gentle touch moved farther down, until his fingers grazed her readied moistness. With a shudder, she laid her head back on the mound of pillows.

She could feel his lips brush the tip of one breast and then the other as he pulled the panties down over her hips. She kept her eyes closed. He was turning back the spread, and removing the rest of his own clothing. After a few seconds, she felt his hands on her face. Opening her eyes, she was surprised to see how solemn his features had become. "Why do you hide your softness, Cara? It's beautiful."

She gazed thoughtfully at his face, saying nothing. A tentative smile played at the corners of her mouth as she looked up into silvery eyes that she could only half see. The glib gentleman was gone. He looked wistful somehow, his voice unsteady. Or was his act just honed to this degree of perfection?

But she wanted to believe it was real. Her body screamed for him. There would be no turning back now.

He entered her with exquisite slowness. Her lips opened in a sigh as he filled her. She lifted her mouth in invitation as he tangled his fingers in her hair. Their kiss was as deep as it was lusty. Cara drew his chest to

hers, and doing so, pulled him more deeply and satis-
fyingly inside her. The sharing of their breaths,
tongues, teeth and heartbeats was a unique sharing. It
thrived and grew.

Martin turned her slightly to her side, his hands
kneading her back, moving up and down, igniting
every nerve ending to a crackling crescendo. Then, almost without warning, his hands moved down to cup
her buttocks, and he pulled her into him. Cara rev-
eled in the delightful sensations that ignited her body
to a fever beyond her wildest dreams. As she cas-
caded over the edge of fulfillment, she arched into
him, crying out her glory at the depth of their joining. Her breath came in small pants as she wound her
legs about his back and clung to him, feeling him hard
and potent within her.

He kissed her throat, his tongue tracing along the
pulsating skin as he pressed her back against the sheet.
He moved away, placing his hands on either side of
her, his knees beneath her thighs.

His silvery eyes glistened with passion, his face
open, unguarded, yet unsmiling, as he pulled himself
almost completely back before he pressed his hips
forward again.

She gasped, clutching his forearms as the thrust of
his hips sent a new, delicious shock wave through her
body. He thrust again, and she felt as though she had
to hold on to him or be thrown off the bed.

His half-closed eyes were gentle and loving as he
judged her reaction. Once again, he went slightly back
to go forward, and her senses careened wildly as she

clutched his arms—two sturdy pillars in her swirling reality.

His slow, perfectly targeted thrusts increased in tempo, and Cara's fingers clawed up toward his shoulders, biting into the corded, sweat-slickened flesh as her panting breaths became passion-wrapped cries.

Her head writhed back and forth as explosion after explosion of liquid fire tore through her. She was filled with the wonder of him to the point of bursting, and she felt herself spiraling upward again to an indescribable brink. Tumbling triumphantly over, she cried out his name over and over, until the sound was little more than a long, sated moan.

Martin covered her with his warmth, enfolding her to him as tears of disbelief glistened in her bright eyes. She embraced him, feeling warm and secure as she held his broad back. Lifting her legs, she circled them about his back and sighed almost sadly, "I...I didn't mean for this to happen."

He kissed her ear, whispering hoarsely, "I did." Lifting his head, he looked down at her face. She was surprised to see his flushed cheeks, and the soft fullness her kisses had given his lips.

"You did?" She felt a vague unease begin to build in her stomach, but couldn't stop herself from tracing a C in the silver hair at his temple. Her lips began a slight trembling as she whispered, "And Martin Dante always gets what he wants." A sorrowful smile tugged at the corner of her lips, and she lifted her gaze past him to stare at the nondescript ceiling, visible in a shaft of yellow light that seeped in from the living room.

Chapter Seven

Most of the time. Yes." His smile was utterly breathtaking as his eyes searched hers.

She stiffened at his callous admission. Staring up at him, she felt suddenly cold and used. Why he looked as proud as any peacock!

An involuntary shiver went through her body. Here she'd done everything in her power to keep this man at arms length, and she'd still ended up dancing to his tune in her own bed! Anger and humiliation seared her face, scalding her skin. If she'd been a tigress, she'd have bared her claws and drawn Dante blood. As it was, she had only words with which to prick his self-satisfied male hide.

She twisted away, ignoring his grunt of discomfort as she wriggled from beneath his considerable weight. "Why you—" she growled "—you conceited bastard! Get the hell out of my house!" She picked up his pants and shirt and flung them toward his bewildered face. "And don't forget your garbage in the kitchen. The next time I want dinner cooked by someone, I'll let Burger King do it. Who needs a piece of a Duke!" She winced, she hadn't meant to say it quite that way.

"Cara..." He reached toward her with a placating hand.

She threw one of his shoes at him, and he batted it to the floor. "Cara, what did I say?"

She picked up his other shoe, but thought better of throwing it just yet. "Put your clothes on, Martin, and get out." It hurt to realize she had let him past her hard fought barriers to take things she hadn't intended to give any man, ever again—especially him! To save face, she blurted cruelly, "You're so damned smug; so damned satisfied with yourself. You think you're such a great lover. Well! As far as I'm concerned, bedroom eyes is all you've got, buster!" Something flared in his silver eyes.

She pointed toward the door with his shoe. "Go! Pick on somebody else!" When he didn't move, she cast her gaze away from his face, unable to meet the leaden glisten of hurt that had settled there.

For a long moment there was no sound. Cara couldn't keep her eyes averted any longer, the silent pull of his pain was too strong. He stood there, stunning in his nakedness, holding both shirt and pants in

one hand, his features closed in a brooding frown.
Feeling very guilty about her cruel lie, *and* angry with
herself for feeling that way, she flung the other shoe to
the carpet at his feet, hissing, "You heard me, Martin. Get out!"

His eyes were vivid and penetrating. "I don't—" he
croaked, then stopped. "Cara—" he shook his head
slowly as he spoke "—I just can't believe you meant
what you said. What we had together just then was—"

"No, Noooo! It wasn't!" She didn't want to hear
the words. What did he want her to do, admit his
mastery over her and kneel at his feet? That's probably what happened after most of his conquests. She
pivoted away, not wanting to stare into those eyes.
Bedroom eyes—bedroom man. She couldn't have him
read the truth in her face. He had too much power
over her. She had to get rid of him, and she had to do
it now—before she was groveling—before she was his
slave!

She lifted her chin, trying to sound totally disinter-
ested. "Why shouldn't I mean it. Men sleep with
woman out of curiosity, don't they?" Now she had to
turn her back on him, discreetly wiping a tear away.
With quick, deliberate movements, she gathered up
her clothes, hurriedly putting them on. "Why...why
shouldn't I?"

He didn't answer. But she could hear the rustle of
his clothes as he dressed. She buttoned the final button of her shirt before she turned back to face him.
"Are you still here?" she demanded a little breathlessly.

He looked up. His eyes lingered on her face for a moment before he let his lashes drop back to mask his eyes. Then he bent to get his tie, muttering flatly, "I'm leaving."

She groaned, running a hand through her hair to try to smooth it. "Please hurry."

His features were composed, but his eyes glittered with emotion as they met hers. It's probably anger, Cara thought or injured male pride. But they were fascinating to behold in the semidarkness. With a suddenness she didn't expect, he turned away. "Goodbye."

She dogged his footsteps into the living room. "Is that all you have to say?" She didn't know why she asked that question. She didn't even know why she had followed him.

When he spun to face her, she almost slammed into his chest. Swallowing, she backed up a step, demanding in a squeaky voice, "Well?"

He scowled at her. The jumping of a muscle in his jaw told her that he was barely controlling his anger as he ground out, "If you want my opinion, I think you're crazy."

She jutted her chin, her eyes glittering with contempt as she hissed back, "Does a woman have to be crazy to resist your charms?"

"Resist?" He lifted a mocking brow. Just then a chime announced that someone was at the door.

Both of them froze at the sound. After a tense moment of silence, there were three heavy thuds on the door.

Cara wailed under her breath, "Who could that be?"

Impatience showed in the brightness of his cool silver eyes as he suggested sardonically, "Your therapist?"

His sarcasm injected steel into her spine, but before she could retort a familiar female voice called, "Cara? Sorry we're early, honey. Cara, are you there?"

Hearing Raleigh's voice, Cara jerked her eyes from Martin's sober face to focus on the door.

"Early?" Martin repeated in a questioning tone, whispering, "It can't be your therapist. If he's anything, he's late."

Cara stared daggers at him, warning between clenched teeth, "Will you shut up? I've got to think."

"Cara? Are you alive or dead?" Evan asked through the door.

Cara's eyes widened, and she pulled her upper lip with her teeth in worried concentration. "What day is it?" She mumbled the question to herself.

His eyes, hard and cold, searched her face. "Wednesday, July sixth. A day that will live in infamy..." He let the statement drop.

"The sixth?" It hit her. "Damn! I got my dates mixed up. How will I ever explain the way I look—or you!" Without waiting for his suggestions, she hurried toward the door. "Yes, Raleigh! Coming!" She flung the door wide, working hard to appear cheerful. "Hi, Ral. Hi, Evan." Stepping back, she allowed them to enter.

A third person followed—a man, tall and lean with sun-bleached, light brown hair that brushed the collar of his tuxedo shirt. His features were strong, almost brooding, but his quick smile softened the intensity of his look and his deep-set blue-green eyes sparkled with humor. "Hi, Cara." He slipped a hand in his pocket, the action making him look every inch an ad for expensive men's wear. When he scanned her attire, he shook his head in faint amusement. "Well, well. You didn't tell me you'd joined a rock group."

"Oh, Donnelly—" she kissed his cheek "—I'm so embarrassed." She thought fast. "I was...uh...cleaning the oven."

"You don't even use the oven, Cara," Evan put in, conversationally. "Now, I might believe you if you said you were hand-grenading it." He raised a questioning brow, but said nothing further in the face of her warning scowl.

She cast an appraising glance at Martin. His expression was unreadable as he watched her. Clearing her throat, she asked with grudging politeness, "Uh...Martin? You know Raleigh and Evan Younger, my sister and brother-in-law, don't you? And Donnelly Wakefield?" She nodded for him. "Um...everybody. Martin just dropped by to pick up his pants—" she grimaced "Uh...that is, I...the other day, spilled wine on them and I had them cleaned and—"

Martin cut her off, extending a hand to Evan, "How are you, Younger?"

"Older every day. And not nearly as comfortable as you." Evan tugged at his tux collar. "Now, you're dressed the way I'd like to be—slacks, open shirt—no belt." He slanted a humorous glance toward Cara.

"You look pretty comfortable, too. Why do I have the feeling you forgot Donnelly's progressive coalition speech tonight?"

"I didn't completely forget, I just got my dates confused." She shrugged helplessly. "I feel like a fool."

Raleigh laughed. "You look like a fool. What a getup. Would you rather we went on without you?"

"No!" She managed a strained smile. "I can change. I don't want to miss it."

"Well, take a little extra time and comb your hair." Raleigh smiled at Cara, but extended a friendly hand toward Martin. "I'm surprised to see you here."

Martin smiled charmingly, taking her hand briefly. "I live below Cara." He said nothing more. But when his eyes shifted toward Cara, she could see that he would have liked to—had he not been raised a gentleman.

Raleigh was surprised. "Oh? She never told me that."

"It wasn't worth mentioning, Ral," Cara replied tightly. She met Martin's gaze with a petulant lift of her chin. "I'll get your pants, Mr. Dante, so that you can be going."

"Dante? Could this possibly be Martin Dante, our computer expert?" Donnelly asked, crossing to Martin with a hand outstretched. "What a nice surprise. I was looking forward to meeting you at our headquarters next week."

As Cara turned to go into her room, she felt an impish stab of inspiration. Throwing a look of pure guile over her shoulder, she called, "Forgive me.

Martin Dante, meet Donnelly Wakefield—our future governor. Why don't you two talk some heavy politics? Martin just loves a good political debate.''

When she returned with Martin's freshly cleaned pants, he was gone. "Where is he?" she rasped.

Evan eyed her curiously. "He said to tell you to give the pants to the Goodwill. But he suggested you keep the groceries. Why was he bringing you groceries?''

A guttural growl in her throat accompanied the clattering of the hanger as it hit the coffee table in front of her couch and then fell to the floor. "Damn him—I don't want his groceries." She glared at them. "Why did you let him go?''

Evan lifted a brow. "Kidnapping is a crime, Cara. Even when it's a man.''

Raleigh hurried to pick up the fallen slacks. "Curly, these look expensive. Don't throw them around.''

"I'll throw them anywhere I want. I paid for having them cleaned.''

"She has a point," Evan quipped, watching her with a strange smile curving one corner of his mouth.

She ground her teeth, turning sparking eyes toward him for a brief instant. She wasn't in the mood to trade fun-loving barbs. Spinning back toward Raleigh, she planted her fists on her hips. "I've got some steaks and Lord knows what else in the kitchen that belong to Martin. After you drop me off tonight, please take it all with you.''

"Uh—thanks.'' Raleigh put the pants down on the couch and took Evan's hand. She looked at him with a helpless lift of her shoulders. "You're the professional here, Younger. What's my sister babbling about?''

He grinned at Cara's livid face, a glint of fun sparkling in his eyes. ''I'd say the lady's angry at the gentleman about something.''

Raleigh groaned. ''Oh, you! Will you never be serious?''

He draped his arm across her shoulders. ''Okay, I'll be serious.'' He slanted a cocked brow at his sister-in-law. ''I don't think Ms. Torrence is happy to discover that Mr. Dante can make her forget what day it is. Anything else—pants and groceries included—is just icing on the cake.''

There was a quiet minute when all three pairs of eyes watched curiously. Shaking with reaction at being talked about as though she was the topic of some lab experiment, she lifted her hands to the sky and curled them into knots. ''Oh Evan, you are so—so dead wrong! For once in your young, inexperienced life, admit it!''

''Okay, Cara, I stand corrected. You just forgot what day it was because *older* people tend to do that. Sorry.'' His twinkling eyes told her he wasn't. Thrusting an elbow in Donnelly's direction, he suggested, ''But right now, could you rustle up something to wear that doesn't look like it's lost a battle? We've got a guest speaker to deliver to several hundred wild-eyed liberals.''

Lost a battle! Why did Evan have to be so on-target? She had, indeed, lost one, tonight—in Martin Dante's arms. As Cara fought valiantly to control the jumbled emotions that had eaten away her poise, Raleigh took her arm. "Sure, Curly. I'll help."

"No." Pulling away, she forced a weak smile. "Thanks, Ral. I'll be ready in a minute." She motioned toward the tray of glasses and bottles on the coffee table. "Why don't you fix yourselves a man while I dress."

"A *man*?" Raleigh repeated incredulously.

Cara stopped, startled at her slip. Evan's laughter kept her from turning around. "I mean a drink." She faked nonchalance as she called back over her shoulder, "By the way, I'm having a birthday dinner for Mom here on Friday. You're all invited. Bring food." When she closed the door to her room, she leaned against the cold wood panels feeling very weary.

Evan lugged two card tables into Cara's condominium. "Okay, chief. The help is here to set up." He leaned the tables against the wall and turned around to grace his hostess with a broad grin. He whistled appreciatively. "Well, well, don't we look feminine for a change."

Cara wrinkled her nose at him. "Evan, you couldn't look feminine if you tried."

"Thank God." He laughed. "Seriously, I like that thing you're wearing."

She lifted a bare shoulder in a careless shrug. "This 'thing' is a strapless jumpsuit." She snapped the stretchy elastic top with her thumb. "Feel free to borrow it anytime. I've always felt that baby blue was your color, Younger." She slipped her hands in the pockets of her blousy pants, and grinned irrepressibly.

He looked at his watch. "Thirteen seconds!" He snapped his fingers. "That's a new record." Looking up at her, he chuckled. "You're pretty sharp—for an old lady."

"Hey. Abbott? Could you and Costello give me some help here?" Raleigh struggled with a hot casserole dish, trying to balance it as she shoved the door open with her shoulder.

"Sure, honey." Evan pulled the door wide. "Need anything else brought in from the car?"

Raleigh headed for the kitchen. "Just the cake. Oh, and a couple of little tablecloths."

Evan laughed in that grand, open way of his. "Cara, love, just out of curiosity, what did you do for this dinner, anyway?"

"I'm donating the roof to eat all Raleigh's birthday cooking under, kiddo. Don't give me any trouble."

He stood in the open door, the hot, early-evening wind ruffling his curly brown hair and the collar of his red knit shirt. "All 'kiddo's' cooking, you mean. What did your folks teach you Torrence girls, anyway?"

"To go after what we want."

He nodded, thoughtfully. "Apparently neither of you wants spatulas or rolling pins very badly."

Cara pointed her finger between his eyes and grinned. "Give that man a cigar!"

He chuckled, brushing her hand away. "I'll get the cake. Why don't you come down with me and get the tablecloths? People in their twilight years need exercise."

She was immediately behind him. "I hope your food is better than your jokes."

As they reached the bottom step, Cara heard the familiar rumble of Martin Dante's car as it turned off the complex's main drive into its parking space. She didn't look at him, but her peripheral vision wouldn't allow the car out of her sight.

"Cara?" Evan nudged her. "Here." He laid the tablecloths in her hands. When she didn't move, he suggested, "You may go now."

She blinked. "Oh..." Pivoting, she headed toward the stairs. Without wanting to, she saw Martin get out of the driver's side of the car and circle around to help someone out—someone shorter and dressed in pale yellow.

With her eyes casting aimlessly about, a casual observer might have believed Cara was scanning the trees for snipers. In truth, she was working desperately not to make eye contact with Martin.

She hadn't seen him since Wednesday night. She'd given the pants—and his belt—to the Goodwill, as he'd suggested. She delighted in the fantasy that when he asked for his belt back, she would have the pleasure of telling him where it was!

Without realizing it, her gaze had swung unconsciously to Martin and his short, yellow-garbed guest just as they reached his door. Catching her searching eyes with his steady ones he nodded, watching her. It was unnerving, that steady, unblinking scrutiny. When she didn't respond, he commented evenly, "Nice evening." He just stood there, holding her in the trap of his eyes, waiting for her to reply. In the pause, the frilly woman turned to look at Cara, apparently interested to see if she was going to agree about the niceness of the evening or not.

Cara swallowed, shifting the tablecloths from one hand to another. "Yes ... I ... it's my mother's birthday."

Martin smiled. It lacked warmth. "I'd love to meet a mother of yours."

"Say, Martin," Evan interjected. "Thanks for the steaks. What were the other things for?"

"Pavlova." One dark brow arched sardonically.

"No kiddin'. I'll make some up tomorrow. I make the best Pavlova ever consumed on this earth. Say—" he seemed suddenly inspired "—speaking of my cooking, why don't you two come up for some cake, later?" Cara could feel the blood drain from her face as Evan went cheerily on, "I baked it, so I know it won't kill anybody. You never know what will happen when the Torrence women are let loose in a kitchen."

Martin's sleepy eyes glittered contemptuously, lingering on Cara as he nodded in agreement. "I can imagine." His lips lifted in a slow grin. It wasn't a friendly expression, but Cara couldn't drag her gaze from the slash of a dimple that tore the perfection of his cheek and gave him the devil-may-care look of a pirate. He murmured easily, "We'd love to, Evan. In about two hours?"

"Great."

Cara felt sick. She couldn't move. Evan's elbow pressed against the small of her back as he whispered out of the corner of his mouth, "Get moving, sport. You look like a department store dummy."

Martin dropped his riveting gaze to sort through his keys. The mechanism in her brain that allowed movements clicked back on, and she hurriedly escaped up the steps. Once inside, she spun to face Evan. She shoved the tablecloths into Raleigh's stomach, and shot back, "Why did you invite him—them—up here for cake, Evan? I hardly know the man, and he can't possibly want to come up here and mingle with a roomful of strangers!"

"Maybe it would be better if Martin doesn't hear this. He might not feel completely welcome." He pushed the door closed with the heel of his loafer and handed Cara the cake. "Martin was free to refuse the invitation, my sweet. He's a big boy. I don't figure he'll be too miserable."

Cara groaned. "What about me? What do you think I'll be?"

His eyes sparkled. "You'll be fun to watch."

The doorbell rang and Cara jumped, absently handing the cake back to Evan. It couldn't be Martin already! Raleigh shook her head at them. "Don't bother, you two, I can see you're busy. I'll get it." She pulled opened the door. "Mom!" With a glad cry, she hugged the chubby woman.

Dixie Torrence's fading blond hair was pulled back in the same neat French roll that she'd worn as far back as Cara could remember. Greatly relieved that it wasn't Martin, she rushed forward to take her mother's hands and pull her into the house. "Hi, Mom. Happy fifty—"

"Thirty-ninth," her father interrupted as he ambled in behind his wife. Lifting his thick glasses off his nose, he wiped them with a handkerchief he'd pulled from his tweedy jacket. "Dixie has decided to try that year again."

Dixie patted Cara's hand. "Yes. As I recall, it was a particularly good one."

Raleigh hugged her mother's plump waist. "I like the dress on you, Mom. I knew aqua would suit you."

Dixie shook her head. "You girls were sweet to give it to me, but you shouldn't have. It's much too expensive."

Raleigh grinned. "Mom, you say that every year."

"Only because it's true. Silk, yet!" She smoothed the fabric lovingly. "Much too expensive!" Dixie touched both of her daughters' faces, smiling. "You both look nice. I like peach on you, Raleigh, but I've never seen a sweater with tiny bowls all over it before. And you, Cara! You and your father need to eat extra cake tonight. Raleigh is thin enough. You and your father are—"

"Well read?" Cara shook her head at her mother. "Mom, if you're through with the traditional preliminaries, shall we sit down?"

"Dad?" Evan asked. "Can I get you a Scotch?"

"Sure, son. Mama?" He took her arm and walked her to Cara's couch. "Would you like a cola or something?"

Dixie eased her bulk onto a cushion. "Love one. I'm parched. Our air conditioning is out on the car again, and getting around in this heat is murder."

"Mine's out too, Mom. I guess that's the Torrence curse. I'll get you that cola." Cara headed toward the kitchen a few steps behind Evan.

"You want me to fix you anything, Cara?" he asked as he poured Scotch into two glasses.

"Uh..." She reached up on tiptoes to get a set of bar glasses from a top shelf. "No, thanks, Evan. I plan to keep a clear head tonight."

"Birthday parties hard on you, usually?"

She put the glasses on the counter and turned to eye him as a rattler eyes a boot in tall grass. "You know why. I'm not looking forward to having Martin Dante here."

"Well then, get drunk, and you'll hardly notice that he's been here at all." He topped the Scotch with soda. "Or do you want to be on your best behavior for some reason?"

"Reasons are your area of expertise, Ev." She handed him two empty glasses and took the full ones, heading toward the living room. "I'll just have soda with a twist of lime. I believe I can trust you to know what Raleigh likes."

"You bet you can. But would you mind asking her what she wants to drink?"

Cara couldn't help but smile. She twisted back to look at him. "Being a psychologist, I bet you're an imaginative fetishist."

He lifted a glass in a silent toast. "We try." When she had turned away, he added, "By the way, Cara,

one of those Scotches in your hand is mine." She
stopped short and turned back to face him. He was
still holding up the glass he'd toasted her with. "This
is your mother's cola." His smile was teasing. "If you
plan to keep a clear head, you're going to have to do
better than this."

"Another helping of casserole, Dad?" Raleigh
dipped the spoon into the broccoli-rice dish as her father made his third trip to the tables.

"Don't mind if I do. Hey, Evan. Raleigh tells me
you made this. It's nigh on the best way I've ever had
broccoli."

Evan put his plate down on the coffee table and
grinned. "It's nigh on the only way I'll have broccoli."

"Raleigh, you come on over and eat, now. You
haven't had a bite." Dixie motioned from her corner
of the couch. "I swear, you and Cara have treated my
birthday dinner like it was poison."

"Not me, Mom. I've been nibbling my way toward
a size twenty. It's Cara we need to pick on. She's
looked a little green all evening."

Cara sat hunched over a plate of food at the opposite end of the couch from her mother. "Don't you
dare. It's not polite to pick on the hostess." Fingering
a carrot stick, she bit off a quarter inch. "See? I'm
eating." If the truth were known, she was nauseated.
Every sound she heard she imagined to be Martin and
his date heading up the stairs. The piece of carrot felt
like a lump of coal in her throat as she looked at her
watch. It was eight thirty-nine.

The knock at the door made her drop her fork. Evan hopped off the stool he was perched on. "I'll get it. Cara, you go on and gather up your utensils."

When she picked up the fork, her shaky fingers let it go again and it clattered to the coffee table. Evan had swung the door wide. "Donnelly, we'd about given you up."

Cara sagged back against the cushion as Donnelly came in, holding a white paper bag. "Sorry I'm so late, but KRMG sent a man by, just as I was leaving, to tape an interview for their ten o'clock report." He added with a grin, "They're doing Mathison tomorrow night."

"With any luck we'll be swallowed up by an earthquake tomorrow afternoon," Cara mumbled as she started to get up to take Donnelly's sack.

With a giggle, Raleigh put a halting hand on her sister's shoulder. "I'll take it, Curly. You eat."

Donnelly pulled a frosty container out of the paper bag. "I brought some vanilla ice cream. I figured it'd go with any flavor of birthday cake Mama Torrence might have."

"Vanilla!" Cara made a face. "And you're supposed to be the liberal candidate? I'd have expected Andrew Mathison to bring vanilla."

"Why, Cara—" Donnelly slid her a taunting glance "—I didn't know he'd been invited."

Everyone laughed at Donnelly's joke as he handed the carton to Raleigh. With a playful scowl toward Cara he added, "You're going to feel terrible when you see what else I brought." He lifted a second carton out of the bag. "Rum raisin. Your favorite."

Evan took the carton. "Oops, afraid not for Cara. She is keeping a clear head tonight."

Cara's glare was lost to his back as Evan exited to the kitchen.

"It was nice of you to bring something, Donnelly," Raleigh commented as she returned from the kitchen.

"When Cara says bring food, I bring food," he returned with a grin. "Besides, I wouldn't miss a chance to be with all of the beautiful Torrence women."

Dixie's shy smile was accompanied by a rush of color. "Oh, Donnelly, you already have my vote. Save your mush."

Raleigh took Donnelly's arm and led him to the serving tables. "I hope you're good and hungry. We've got tons of food."

"Starved. Haven't had time to eat all day." Donnelly picked up a plate. "It looks great."

"Thanks." Evan came back in and gave Donnelly a comradely pat on the back. "It was nothing any competent master chef couldn't have done."

Amid a burst of laughter, another knock sounded at the door. Cara froze. There was nobody left who might drop by—except Martin and his frilly friend. She pushed her plate of cold food off her knees onto the coffee table. The action made her fork slide off the table and onto the floor again. Evan strode quickly to the door, calling over his shoulder, "Somebody go get Cara more silverware while I see who this might be."

"What in heaven's name, Cara? You certainly have the 'droppies' tonight." Dixie leaned across her husband to make the remark. It seemed excessively loud in the expectant room. Cara made no attempt to answer over the anxious lump in her throat. Her eyes were glued to the door that Evan was opening.

"Martin Dante! Well, come on in." Evan backed away as Martin allowed his companion to precede him.

"Nice of you to invite us." Martin shook Evan's hand. Cara couldn't help but notice how striking he looked, all silver, white and black. He'd taken off his coat and vest. His white shirt was open at the neck where a sprig of black hair contrasted sharply. She swallowed with difficulty, remembering how it felt under her hands—and her lips.

His hair seemed blacker as indirect lighting caught and favored its silver accent; and the glisten in his mercury eyes mirrored the sheen of silver in his suit pants. She had to admit he was a gorgeous man. She reminded herself, Yes, he's gorgeous, rich, spoiled, superior, unfeeling, superficial and an awesome lover—she ground her teeth. Where had *that* come from?

His voice interrupted her mental turmoil. "I'd like to introduce a friend of mine. Jane Connerly."

So this was a Jane Connerly, Cara thought darkly. She was definitely not the girl Martin had been in the park with on the Fourth. This woman was well endowed, equally young, equally attractive, and for some reason, Cara took an instant dislike to her.

Martin scanned the group as he said something to Cara's mother, but Cara wasn't catching the words. She was watching his face. She noticed that when he saw Donnelly, his smile faded slightly. Naturally, Cara decided, he would prefer not to be around one political side when he was working for both. But he must have realized this party would be a hotbed of Wakefield sympathizers!

His eyes shifted back to her, and he extended a hand. "And this is our hostess, Jane. Cara Torrence."

Cara lifted her chin, offering the young woman a hostessy smile. "It's lovely to meet you, Jane." She shifted in her seat, pushing herself up to perch on its edge. She could feel herself stiffening, so she attempted to look relaxed by throwing a casual elbow along the arm of the couch. "So...Jane. You in Martin's computer class?" She winced inwardly. Why did she ask that? Who cared?

Jane took the seat offered by Evan, smoothing her skirt over her knees. "Why, no. We know each other through TRAC—you know, Tulsa Racquetball and Aerobics Club?"

"Yes." Cara nodded. "I teach rhythmic aerobics there."

Jane looked surprised. "Oh? You're her? I've heard of your classes."

Cara propped her chin on a fist. "Why don't you join us?"

Jane shook her dark head, smiling sweetly. "Oh, I'm into jogging, right now. That's how I met Mart. He's trying to talk me into entering the Tulsa Run in October."

Cara's glance shifted to meet his eyes as he stood behind Jane's chair. "Oh? Well, don't let him talk you into anything you don't want to do."

Martin raised a brow.

Jane laughed. "I'll try not to. But he's very persuasive. And what a cook! He just fixed the most wonderful steaks I've ever tasted."

An unexpected shaft of dismay slid through her at Jane's words. She tried to pull her gaze from Martin's face, but his eyes held hers relentlessly as a vague smile curved one corner of his mouth. "Why, thank you, Jane," he said, touching her shoulder. She turned to smile up at him.

With some effort Cara managed to pull her gaze away. Determined not to remember what had happened two nights ago when he'd brought steaks to her apartment, she veered away from the subject as casually as she could, "Actually, Jane—" she cleared her squeaky throat "—uh, my rhythmic aerobics classes could help you train for the run. And with the music, it's not boring, like jogging is."

Martin chuckled deep in his throat, drawing Cara's gaze. "What's so funny?" she asked through thinned lips.

He shrugged; the perceptive glance he gave her held a baiting quality. "Don't sell her a bill of goods, Cara. Your little dancing class couldn't possibly prepare a person for a nine mile run."

She blinked at him in disbelief, feeling as though he'd slapped her face. Her lips opened, but she couldn't find appropriately stinging words to express her opinion of his glaring ignorance.

"Say, Martin? How about something to drink?" Evan stepped in, putting a hand on his shoulder. "And Ja—"

"He doesn't drink, Evan!" Cara snapped, her eyes never leaving Martin. "What do you mean, couldn't possibly prepare a person for a nine mile run!" she demanded, belatedly finding her voice.

Martin gave her a level glance. "Cara, the Tulsa Run is fifteen kilometers of bone-grinding punishment. It's run outside, in heat, rain or cold, and let's not forget wind. It's around an hour of running at an exhausting pace. You women jump around a gym looking cute. There's nothing cute or graceful about running nine miles."

"Cute!" Cara shot to her feet. "Is that what you think aerobic dancing is? Cute?"

Evan stepped in front of Martin to face his livid sister-in-law. "Oh, good. Our hostess is up and ready to get the cake."

She flung her brother-in-law a black look. But he had turned back to face Jane and Martin. "Now, what would you two like to drink? I'm brewing coffee."

Cara felt Raleigh's hand on hers and turned to face her sister. Raleigh's expression was closed in worry. In a hushed whisper she cautioned, "It's Mom's birthday party, Curly. Let's not turn it into a debate. Please!" she pleaded. "Especially with Martin Dante. It wouldn't do to antagonize him."

"Antagonize him!" Cara gritted. "He started it!"

"You started it, calling jogging boring. What did you expect him to say?" Cocking her head toward the kitchen, she asked a little more loudly, "Show me where you keep your cake knife?"

"If he's not careful I'm going to keep it between his ribs!" Cara rasped back as she was hauled into the kitchen. The man thought he knew so much. How dare he belittle her aerobics classes. Someday, she vowed, he'd fall off that high horse and she'd damn well be there pulling him by the leg!

"On second thought, you get the dessert plates." Raleigh gave Cara a good-natured shove toward the pantry. "Better make them paper plates. I'll find something nice·and dull to cut the cake with."

Chapter Eight

Darn that man!'' Cara dashed up the stairs to the aerobic workout room, five minutes late. Why had Martin had to come home this afternoon just as she was about to leave? She'd been so busy doing work for the upcoming primary election she hadn't laid eyes on him for three weeks. But today he'd arrived early, and he'd seemed to be purposely taking forever to go inside, piddling around his car just when she had to get to the club to teach her class!

She'd spent more time simmering and stewing over him in these past weeks than she cared to admit. All the more reason not to be anywhere near him. She had no intention of getting back on that merry-go-round again, leaving herself open and totally vulnerable. She mumbled, "Make me a fool once, shame on you.

Make me a fool twice, shame on me." Not a *third* time. She nodded with her firm conviction. Not for Cara Torrence. She would be *nobody's fool*, ever again!

Dressed in a skinny pink leotard and mauve tights and leg warmers, she had paced nervously back and forth before her door, every few seconds pivoting with a squeak of her aerobic shoes toward the window to check to see if he'd left. He hadn't. Finally, she'd heaved a sigh as desolate as an August wind. She had to leave, Martin Dante or no. Flinging open her door, she dashed down the stairs, trying to keep her eyes off him as she headed toward her Pinto.

Hearing her pad down the steps, Martin had looked up from the open trunk, a trunk that from Cara's window had nothing but microscopic computer parts undetectable to the human eye. Unbidden, her eyes had roamed to meet his. When they'd made contact, a half smile lit his face. Even a pseudopleasant look from him was enough to stun more receptive women. "Off to aerobics?" he'd asked rhetorically as his eyes took in her costume. "Have fun . . . jiggling."

Refusing to be intimidated by his belittling comment, she tossed her head in carefree dismissal and jumped into her car. The memory of him standing there, tall and lean, framed in her rearview mirror, lingered in her mind as she bounded around a corner on the upper floor of the TRAC toward thirty women milling and visiting in the large, carpeted room, waiting for class to start.

Putting Martin Dante firmly on a back shelf of her mind, she greeted them with a hearty wave. "I'm sure you've already stretched out. So let's get to it. I can almost hear the fat accumulating!'' She hurried to the sound system and inserted the first tape. ''Everybody down for sit-ups.''

''What about everybody up for sit-downs?'' a familiar voice asked flippantly. ''I'm too fat to do anything else just now.''

Cara stilled, her head bent over the tape recorder. Lifting her gaze toward the mirrored wall, she looked into the smiling blue eyes of one of her longtime students, and class cutup, Lucy Dunn.

Lucy nodded. ''It's been a while, but you're looking as great as ever.''

One corner of Cara's mouth lifted. ''Hi, Lu. I heard through the grapevine you were pregnant again. You didn't have to quit coming to class.'' She dropped the tape into place and flicked the switch to Rewind. ''Don't you remember me telling you that babies born to women in rhythmic aerobic classes have slower heartbeats than average babies?''

''Not the way I exercised, hon. Remember? I'm the one who took candy bar breaks in the middle of class.''

''As I recall, you never were exactly driven.'' Turning to face Lucy, she grinned. ''But I didn't think you'd go to this extreme to get out of doing sit-ups.'' Motioning to the women to quit chatting and get down on their mats, she asked, ''When's number five due?''

''Five and six.'' Lucy grinned at Cara's wide-eyed surprise. ''It'll be my third set of twins—and they'll arrive in a couple more weeks.'' She patted her stomach. "Next time I don't plan to be in my ninth month in August. Too damned hot!"

"Next time! Geeeez!" Cara rolled her eyes. "Don't tell me, tell Larry. Listen, can you hang around so that we can talk after class?"

Lucy nodded, her thick brown hair bouncing casually about her shoulders. "Why not? Larry's at home with the rest of the brood. I escaped for the evening. Bert and Ernie have the flu, and Attila and Godzilla are going through puberty. Not a pretty sight."

"You nut." Cara laughed as she switched the tape to Play and dropped to the mat. Smiling up at Lucy she motioned to the weight training equipment that took up half of the long room. "Go find some place to sit. I'll buy us a couple of orange juices after class." Raising her voice so that it would carry over the upbeat tune, she called out, "Okay, girls, let's flatten those stomachs. Curl up—one—two—"

The session started amid groans and laughter. That was the way Cara liked to keep her students—working and laughing. That way, the hour of stretching, toning and dancing flew by. Thirty minutes into the aerobics workout, she looked down at her wristwatch, instructing loudly. "Count your pulse for six seconds. Keep moving!" Her eyes flitted to the other side of the room. The weight-lifting equipment always got popular with the men when the woman's aerobics class was in progress. Some of the women resented their intrusion, some enjoyed it. Cara, on the whole, ignored it. She had to or she couldn't concentrate on the memorized steps. "Okay, stop! I hope everyone is watching their heart rate and obeying their body's messages. Do as much as you can, but don't overdo." She flipped the tape over. "*Maniac* is next. Ready?"

As the music began, several of the newer students moaned and staggered to lean against the wall or flop to the carpet out of the way of flying feet. Cara was leading the class into the most strenuous group of aerobic exercises.

At one point, she twirled around and caught sight of Lucy leaning against some weight equipment. She was talking to a tall man. But all Cara could glimpse of him was a muscular arm and part of a white net T-shirt. Twirling away, she dismissed them from her mind as she led the workout into its final phase.

After the cool-down routine was over, Cara had the class check their pulses again to insure that they were all dropping back to a normal heart rate as they were supposed to. She picked up a towel and patted her forehead, pushing back damp curls. With a cooling shake of her hair, she draped the towel about her neck and headed toward Lucy. Since the continuing education classes at TU didn't meet in August, she needn't hurry away; they'd have plenty of time to visit.

Rounding the maze of sparkling weight equipment, she was about to speak when her eyes were captured in a blue-white snare. Her invitation to get juice was vaporized by the white heat of his look.

When Martin's gaze shifted from Lucy's face to somewhere beyond her head, Lucy turned. "Hi, Cara. I'd like you to meet a friend of mine." She turned to face the paralyzed Cara, touching Martin's arm casually. "This is Martin Dante. He took his father's place as chairman of the board of Tulsa Exchange Bank last year." Lucy slanted Martin a half-reproving look. "So far he's neglected to make Larry a vice president, but—" she patted her stomach "—I'm sure he will soon. It's the least he can do for the children."

Cara sniffed derisively. "Why? Are they his?"

Lucy's jaw sagged, and Martin burst out laughing. He draped a casual arm about Lucy's shoulders. "Don't mind Cara, Lucy. She's just trying to tell you in her own quaint way that we've already met, and she's crazy about me."

Lucy looked from one to the other. "Ooooohhh?" Her nonplussed expression softened into a smile of titillated interest. "I'm happy for you, Martin. Cara eats most men for breakfast."

Martin's sleepy eyes glittered. "I know." Very slowly his gaze moved over her stiffened features.

"Except maybe for Donnelly Wakefield," Lucy added, oblivious to the tensions between her two companions.

Martin didn't take his eyes off Cara, his tone level. "Is that so?"

Lucy giggled. "Yes, Donnelly's every woman's pinup right now. It's amazing what a pretty face on a political poster can do to otherwise sane women." She flipped a negating hand toward Cara. "Of course Ms. Torrence doesn't fall in that category much of the time."

Martin grunted and murmured something more to himself than anyone. It sounded like "Here, here."

Cara paid no attention to Lucy's joke or Martin's mumbled agreement. Leaving one hand grasping a supporting bar of the military press machine, she planted a fist on her hip, cutting her eyes to Lucy. "That's awful! You shouldn't talk about a wonderful, caring man like Donnelly so flippantly! You know he's just the man we need to be our governor!"

Lucy cast a sidelong glance up at Martin. "I love to do that."

Martin's eyes narrowed with curiosity. "What?"

Lucy shrugged. "Get her mad. Makes up for all the times she's nearly killed me on the aerobics floor."

Cara forced herself to move closer. The immediate shock of seeing Martin had lessened, and she decided that she must look ridiculous hugging the corner of the heavy piece of equipment.

She adjusted her posture to a casual stance, ignoring Martin. She smiled sheepishly at Lucy. "So now we're even. Why don't we go get that juice?" Gathering her courage, she eyed Martin with what she hoped looked like extreme disinterest. "If you'll excuse us, Martin, I'm sure we're keeping you from your jogging, or racquetball—or something?"

He shook his dark head. "No, actually, Cara, you're the reason I'm here." In his pause, her pulse began to race wildly. Oh *no*! She didn't want to be a reason he was *anywhere*! She felt her cheeks go hot as he continued, "I wanted to let you know about some software the club will be testing for a while. Your class would benefit from it."

She stared up at him, waiting for him to explain.

"Actually, Dennis gave me the idea." One corner of his mouth lifted in a wry half smile. "You remember Dennis—the gun slinging sophomore?"

Cara eyed him warily. "What about him?"

"I visited him at his home a couple of weeks ago and discovered that he was into nutrition and exercise. He's working on a program designed to help people devise balanced meals and determine the number of calories needed to change or maintain weight. Dennis was frustrated about a couple of bugs he couldn't work through, so we put our heads together and came up with a program we're calling Fit-Calc." He paused, savoring the glint of interest that came to life in Cara's eyes. "It lists all the proteins, carbohydrates, fats, calories, sodium, fiber fluid, vitamin and mineral content—as well as calories—for over one thousand different foods. And it allows you to feed in five hundred additional food items of your choice."

Lucy interjected, "Wow, Cara. Sounds like a miracle for people floundering in the maze of faulty diet information that's flooding the market lately."

Cara's gaze didn't move from Martin's eyes, but she nodded. "Yes. I . . . I'd like to know more." What she didn't say was that she didn't want to learn it from Martin.

He nodded his head in the direction of the stairs. "Dennis has the software down in the office. We've already given them the stipulation that other club members can only use the program after you and your classes get first crack at it."

"Hmm." Lucy crossed her arms over her stomach and eyed both of them. "Interesting stipulation."

Cara swallowed. This was a distressing turn of events, but then she couldn't deny her loyal students the information. She admitted, "Well, it certainly sounds like something the women would love to have." She frowned. "Why the stipulation? Why not let Jane and your other precious joggers have first crack at it?"

"It was Dennis's stipulation. Fit-Calc was basically his idea." The set of Martin's shoulders was a dismissal. "And he's fond of you."

She cringed at his emphasis on the word "he's." Darn that Dennis, anyway! Why couldn't he have worked the bugs out on his own and kept Martin out of it? Without much enthusiasm, she mumbled, "I see. I'll thank him." She hoped he noticed her emphasis on the word "him." She was feeling weak in the knees again being this close to Martin and she didn't like it.

He motioned toward the dance area. "The nutrition program, along with your aerobics class would probably make a fairly complete fitness program—" his eyes lit with devilry "—as complete as one can get by jiggling, that is."

Lucy twisted her head around toward Martin. "Oh-oh." She reached out and patted his cheek. Pity twisted her lips in a sad smile. "Well, Martin. It's been nice knowing you." She cocked her head toward Cara. "I can't look. Tell me, is there smoke coming out of her ears yet?"

Martin's white teeth flashed in a quick, beautiful grin. He was a devil, straight out of hell! Cara's mouth froze in a straight line of barely suppressed fury.

"Lucy," she rasped, "go see if the vending machine is out of guns."

Lucy giggled delightedly. "This is my cue to leave, Martin." She patted his cheek again. "My condolences, chief. I hope you left Larry that vice presidency in your will."

Martin's gaze followed Lucy's retreat for a moment before he turned back to face Cara. The corners of his mouth lifted. "Lucy's a character—"

"Jiggling!" Cara exploded, wild-eyed and flushed. She wanted to do him physical violence. Never in her life had she wanted to leap onto a man more than this man at this moment—to get her hands on him and . . . "How dare you use that word over and over again! It's insulting!"

He lifted his powerful shoulders, the muscles flexing in a shrug. "It was your word."

She took a threatening step forward. They were now so near that she could feel his warm breath on her forehead. She lifted a defiant chin. "Well, I'm getting sick of hearing *you* say it!"

His lazy lids lifted in feigned surprise. "You called jogging boring."

"It is boring. It's mindless miles of monotonous ground-pounding!"

"Mindless miles of . . ." He let the sentence drop and whistled long and low. "You don't think much of jogging, do you?"

Her voice was rising with her anger. "It's not so much jogging I hate, it's the narrow-mindedness of the men who do it! Do you have any idea how many times I've heard men up here snicker about our workouts?

Why, I bet I could run circles around them. Including you!"

"Cara." He reached out and touched her shoulder. "Take it easy. There's no point in getting hysterical—"

She brushed his hand away. "Hysterical, am I!" she shrieked. She was tired—very tired of the kind of things men said belittling the importance of what she taught. For nearly six years she'd heard the snide remarks; they were ignorant, stupid comments straight from the macho mentality, and she'd had enough.

Her mind burned with a thousand asinine remarks, and Martin's put-down was the last straw! Finally, too angry to stop herself, she blurted out a challenge. "I'll make a bet with you, Martin Dante!" She thumped him on the chest with a finger, emphasizing each word. "I bet you that I can beat you in the Tulsa Run this October. I'll beat you and I'll never do anything to prepare for it but teach my regular classes here!"

"What?" Shaking his head, he rejected the idea completely. "No, Cara." He took her abusing hand into his. "That's crazy. It wouldn't be fair to you."

"Not fair to me!" She jerked out of his hold and balled her hands at her sides. "What kind of cop-out is that?"

He looked disturbed. "The run's fifteen kilometers—nine miles, Cara. Do you have any idea how long nine miles—"

She blustered, "Don't talk down to me, Martin. Don't you dare. I've danced for five hours straight at aerobics clinics. Nine miles doesn't take anywhere near five hours."

He flexed his jaw. "For some, it could."

"Not me."

He pursed his lips, his frown deepening. "Cara, you can't beat me. Men can run faster than women. And I'm pretty good."

"So you say." She squared her shoulders. "Does that mean you intend to win the race?"

"Win?" He grunted out a humorless chuckle. "Of course not. I'll leave that to the kids training for the Boston Marathon and the Olympics."

"And have you forgotten? You're three years older than I am."

His eyes narrowed. "Thanks."

She'd hit a chord that time. A smirk of superiority lifted her lips, bolstering her courage to go on. "Besides, even though men are faster, women are traditionally better when it comes to endurance. I'd say nine miles takes plenty of that."

"Oh, Cara," he urged tiredly, spreading his hands. "Think about what you're getting yourself into."

"I've thought about it all I need to. And, I just *dare* you to try and beat me!"

He dropped his hands. "Is there any way I can deal with you logically, or are you going to rave on no matter how much I try to reason with you?"

"Rave on?" Pride pushed her nose toward the sky. Lifting slender brows in offended skepticism, she dared him. "Why don't we just see?" She snapped her head in a positive nod, her eyes holding his levelly. "Why don't we just see what you think about my 'jiggling' classes after I beat you. You'll be sorry you ever heard the word."

"I'm already sorry."

She crossed her arms before her, feeling positive about her ability to win. "Aha! Admitting failure already?"

Mercury lightning flashed beneath the deceptively drowsy gaze. Running a distracted hand through his hair, he exhaled heavily. One side of his mouth curled down in an intriguing expression of self-disgust. "Damn it, Cara. Cut it out. I don't like dares." His words grated to a halt, and he forced his glittering eyes away from her compact sweetness to roam over the weight-training equipment.

She could see a surly twitch begin to kick along the strong line of his lean jaw. He was angry. The darkened, sharp planes of his profile fascinated her. Why did this man have to be so exciting to her senses?

The only sound that Cara could hear in the large room was the labored breathing of one lone man, straining to pull down a weighted bar to shoulder level. Dragging her eyes away from Martin's scowling profile, she silently watched the flexing of the man's glistening arm and shoulder muscles. In the tense quiet, she began to count his slow, rhythmic grunts. There had been five, when Martin's irritated growl made her jump. "Damn it, woman, I tried. It's a bet." When he turned back to face her, his nostrils flared with his resentment at having been placed in this position. "Fifty bucks too steep for you? I hate to take your money. But you asked for this."

She took a step closer to him, hissing, "Oh, no, you don't. You could lose fifty dollars without batting an eye." Her voice was barely more than a whisper as she

said, "I'm going to make it harder on you than that."
She tossed her head, and pulled the towel from around
her neck. "When you lose the race, you come up
here...." She flipped the towel toward the dance area.
A small part of her brain reserved for inconsequential
matters recorded the fact that the man who had been
working out was leaving. Wagging the towel under
Martin's nose, she went on. "You dance with us for an
hour. I promise you'll be screaming for mercy when
you get finished."

His expression was thoughtful as he pulled her terry
weapon from her fingers. His lack of panic irritated
her, so with hardly a pause, she added insult to injury. "And you'll have to wear a clown suit during the
class—red nose and all!"

"Hmm." Looping the towel back over her shoulder, he appeared to assimilate that news. After a moment, his concentrated expression changed to an
unsettling grin. "Okay. Fine." Before she was aware
of it, he had smoothed the towel down over her
breasts, his hands brazenly intimate in the brief time
they lingered.

Anticipating correctly that she would back away
from his touch, he halted her by clamping both of his
hands on her shoulders. His light eyes glittering with
masculine determination, he leaned forward so that
they were nose to nose, eye to eye, and very nearly lip
to lip. The whispered demand he made was exceptionally husky. "And when you lose, my pigheaded
little dreamer, you will come home from the race with
me and cater to my every whim...." He watched her
expression fade from smug superiority to abject hor-

ror as he went on casually. "And don't underestimate the word cater." His eyes took on a satanic glint and she winced as he enumerated, "You'll cook for me, you'll fetch for me—you'll do *everything* I ask of you, for twenty-four hours."

She wondered if he thought it was escaping her attention that, after each addition to the list, he had pulled her slightly closer to him. They were now so close that she could feel the heat of his body against her skin. She put out a halting hand. Pressing it against his hard chest she could feel the heavy, even beat of his heart as she gasped distractedly. "No." It was said so softly that she was not sure he heard it, though it was echoing like the blast of a cannon in her mind.

Cater to him? Be with him for twenty-four hours! Absolutely not! Never! Pulling wildly out of his hold on her, she raked both hands through her hair, rejecting the proposition in a shivery moan. "I won't do it. I only asked you for an hour. How can you ask me for twenty-four?"

His wide, sensuous mouth lifted mockingly, and the steely hardness in his eyes gave her even less hope of a reprieve, as he said, "There were no limits mentioned about time—only money." He reached out and touched one of the damp curls that clung to her forehead. "It's a good bet, Cara. Neither one of us has any intention of doing what the other demands. So, we'll fight to the death."

She jerked away from his touch. "For once, we agree. I'd rather die than spend twenty-four hours with you."

A shadow of emotion darkened the steel color of his eyes. "You want to back out?"

"Not on your life." She took a step backward. "I'll beat you into the earth!"

He smiled coolly. "Does that mean you won't cook dinner for me tonight?"

Cara's lips parted in amazement. Finding her voice with some difficulty, she threw back, "Bright lad!"

"Later, then." He seemed so sure. That bothered her. He turned away, and with an easy grace straddled the leg press machine, settling into the seat. She barely caught his low murmur as he adjusted the tension. "And the software? Is your pigheadedness going to keep your class from benefiting from it?"

She frowned. The nutritional program was important. Making her decision, she answered as calmly as she could considering her mental turmoil. "I'll go talk to Dennis about it, if you promise you won't join us."

Arching a brow, he surprised her with an arrogant grin. "You're going to need me."

Turning abruptly, she headed toward the stairs, calling back defiantly, "If I do, I'll just bang my fist against a wall until the urge goes away!"

"That seems to be a way of life for you—banging your fists against walls," he goaded, the low remark heavy with sarcasm.

She bared her teeth in a carnivorous smile. "Martin." The harsh, ragged sound that darkened her voice stilled every muscle in his body, and he sat watching her, unmoving, unsmiling, straining to hear her whispered edict. "Let me make my intentions clear. I will— very reluctantly—see you in October at the race. Until then, I'll be working on Donnelly's campaign. In consideration of the sensitivity of your job—and my all-consuming dislike for you—I think it will be better if we don't see each other between now and then.''

With a burning face, she turned and ran; her hair whipped her face, stinging her eyes. She reached the steps in three long strides and flailed blindly, grabbing the handrail as though it were a lifeline. With both hands sliding along the rail, she bounded down the stairs two at a time, her heart pounding like a sledgehammer. Tears sparkled on her lashes, and she blinked to clear her vision. A suffocating feeling of loss tightened her chest and made her breathing difficult. What was it she felt so clearly? Was she already anticipating her defeat in the run—or was it something else?

Chapter Nine

Martin cursed under his breath as he heard his hubcap hop the curb and roll into the darkness. He braked the car. At least it had waited to fall off until he got home. Small favor. He rummaged in his glove compartment for his flashlight. It wasn't there. "Damn!" he muttered, as he slid out and slammed the door, heading off after it.

It was well after midnight, and this was all he needed to top off a perfect day! The last thing he wanted to be doing was kicking around in the woods after a lump of chrome. He squinted, scanning the deep shadows, but his mind was not really on his hubcap. He kept visualizing the television screen tonight, when he'd seen Donnelly and Cara in an intimate tête-à-tête as cameras had scanned Wakefield headquarters during coverage of the primary election.

He muttered a curse unworthy of even a drunken sailor and kicked a tree. Why did that little hellcat have to make him feel jealous? He shook his head and put an arm around the tree trunk as though asking for its forgiveness. "She eats men for breakfast, you know—unless maybe they're going to be governor! Then she's all soft and smiling." Like tonight. His jaw worked in irritation at the memory. She'd been wearing something pink and silky that had brushed against Donnelly with every wispy breeze. Martin turned his forehead to the bark, closing his eyes. With Donnelly, even Cara's clothes flirted. With him, she shot to kill.

The woman wasn't so crazy, she was just wily as a fox. She knew what she wanted. And she'd made it painfully clear that it wasn't Martin Dante. She was going after bigger game. Maybe the biggest. The thought passed his mind that governor was only the beginning for Wakefield. A low rumble in his chest was the only sound in the stillness as he laughed in self-disgust at his foolish weakness for such an improbable creature as Cara Torrence!

He'd never had to go out and get drunk over a woman before. Not until tonight. But when he'd seen Cara, smiling at Donnelly, he'd tried to get drunk; tried to forget about the fire in her touch and in her eyes—a fire that made him feel warm and really alive for the first time in his life.

Damn that woman! You couldn't deal with her unemotionally, coolly. She was all emotion—one hundred proof passion! You spent five minutes with her and you were staggering around holding your head! And what was worse, she was addictive. She'd kept him awake nights, tossing and turning, wanting more of her charged spirit in his life. Why didn't she wear a surgeon general's warning label—Kissing This Woman Could Be Hazardous To Your Sanity.

He couldn't figure out exactly why she thought she had to be so tough. She'd either been hurt badly by someone, or she was so cunning and conniving about the man she wanted, she was willing to step over a lot of male bodies to get him. If that was true, then the "him" she wanted was Donnelly Wakefield. That fact was painfully obvious.

He dropped his hand from the tree and walked away. His foot hit something metallic, and he reached down to investigate. "There you are, you piece of—"

The sound of a motor made him tense, and he turned toward the parking lot. It was Evan's car. He relaxed a little. Raleigh and Evan were bringing Cara home. The last thing he wanted to see was Donnelly Wakefield walk up those steps and disappear into her apartment. He wasn't sure they were sleeping together. But, damn! Wakefield was the only man she ever smiled at. If she slept with anyone, it was probably he. And any woman of her fiery nature was certainly sleeping with someone.

He ran a hand over his eyes, stepping into the shadows. He felt as foolish as a schoolboy spying on the girl next door, but he didn't move. The car door opened, and he could see Cara as she got out, that pink dress swirling and dancing on the warm breeze.

Her laughter was light and soft as she waved Raleigh and Evan away.

His lips curved up in self-mockery. He could almost believe she knew he was out there, and that she was torturing him with her indifference. She stepped onto the sidewalk and moved like night mist toward the stairs. In a moment she would be gone. His nostrils flared and his palms began to sweat. If he'd been an alcoholic, he'd have run for a bottle. As it was, he began to move toward her. He couldn't let her walk away from him, not again. He wanted another chance.

Cara waved again to Raleigh and Evan as their car disappeared around the corner of her condominium parking area. She was tired. Every bone in her body ached. But, aching bones or no, Cara smiled. Donnelly had won the primary. She lifted the thin strap of her purse to her shoulder, her brows furrowing in a slight frown as she recalled how Raleigh had repeatedly praised Martin's perfect predictions of the outcome. As far as Raleigh was concerned, Martin Dante could do no wrong. Cara paused at the base of the steps to her condominium and sighed audibly. She might be able to fault him about some things, but not about his work. He'd computed Donnelly's share of the vote to be fifty-seven percent. His share had been just that when the other two candidates conceded the primary victory to him.

"Congratulations."

Cara's foot froze on the first step and she scanned the darkness. The only illumination came from a slice of moon that peeked through the rustling branches of ancient oaks that surrounded the Landmark condo-

miniums. Because she recognized Martin's deep bari-
tone voice, she didn't panic, but even so, her body
stiffened.

"Thanks." She looked around, asking in a slightly
strained whisper, "Where are you?"

"Here." A vague movement near a gnarled oak ten
feet away caught her eye as Martin stepped out of the
shadows.

Cara leaned against the railing. "I see. The question now is, why are you out there?"

The crunch of late-summer grass grew louder as he
walked up the gradual incline toward the sidewalk. "I
just got home." He held up something large and
round, glinting like metal. "Lost a hubcap."

Cara sniffed out a short laugh. "I thought Mer-
cedeses regenerated the parts they shed."

Martin tucked the disk under one arm and came
around to lean against the opposite rail. He ignored
her sarcasm, remarking quietly, "I saw you on television—you and Donnelly." He inclined his head toward her. "You look very nice tonight."

She didn't know what to say to him. She'd prepared to be brusque and go on her way if she happened to run into him this way, but somehow his mild
tone and somber mood—and possibly the moon-
light—made her want to linger.

"Thank you, Martin." She could make out his face
now that her eyes were becoming accustomed to the
darkness. He looked troubled. And he smelled—
strange. She wrinkled her nose. "Martin, where have
you been? You smell like a brewery." His eyes glistened like torches in the darkness as they roamed over

her, and she felt uncomfortably warm under their touch.

"Bar," he murmured.

"Bar?" Her jaw dropped when she realized what he meant. "You mean—*a bar*? *You?*"

"Yeah. I got...tired of watching the primaries. There was no question about...about the winner by ten o'clock." He sat down on a step. Before he spoke, he leaned the hubcap against the slatted railing. "Decided to play a couple of games of pool."

"Pool!" She forced a nervous laugh. "I thought you were programmed for polo."

He ran a hand through his hair and leaned forward, resting his forearms on his knees. Sounding tired, he said, "Cara—don't."

She frowned. This was not the Martin Dante she knew. He looked something like him in those expensive navy suit pants and the starched white, button-down shirt. The tie was gone, however, and the shirt had been unbuttoned to about mid chest. His hair was, well, not quite perfect. There was a wisp that hung down over his forehead. She had to quell the urge to reach down and smooth it into place.

Not caring to search very deeply for the reason why she chose to do it, she sat down beside him. He seemed oddly vulnerable. She reached out to touch his face, but stopped herself just in time, gritting her teeth at her softening. Dropping her hand, she observed dryly, "You're not a fun drunk, Martin."

"I'm not drunk. It might be better if I were," he said enigmatically. "Some woman spilled her beer on me."

She shifted on the step to look at his face. "Some..." She let the sentence die away. It wasn't her business whom he went to bars with.

He finished for her. "Woman." One corner of his mouth lifted in a weary half grin. "*She* offered to have it laundered, too."

Cara felt a tremor run up her spine. A jealousy she could never have anticipated gripped her heart like a fist around a flower, crushing, killing it. Though she fought the feeling, her throat closed. She wondered if he realized how badly he was hurting her by telling her this.

Abruptly standing, she floundered for a way to make as rapid an exit as possible. "Well...I'm... happy for you, Martin. If your luck continues, you'll never have to do your own laundry again." She cleared her throat to ease the tenseness that had sharpened her words.

He frowned up at her. "I'm happy you're so happy." As he said it, he stood. When he had straightened, they were eye to eye, with Martin standing on the pavement and Cara balanced precariously on the second step.

With a supporting hand gripping the rail, she lifted her heel to the step behind her, preparing for flight. "Isn't it fine that we're both so happy...."

When she whirled away, he reached out and took her hand. "Cara. I'm still wearing the shirt."

She turned back to look at him. His expression was searching, intense as he held her gaze with his. "Don't go." His whisper was husky, almost pleading. The silvery glow of his eyes in the darkness had a mesmerizing effect on her, and she hesitated. She wanted to stay more than anything she had ever wanted in her life. If only she could lay down her arms and come into his.

But that was the very trap she was trying to avoid— and Martin Dante was a dangerous, tantalizing trap, with broad shoulders and a kiss that could level cities. One slip with him, and she'd be a doormat for his every demand. And she couldn't allow that to happen to her again! Very slowly, very reluctantly she pulled her hand from the inviting warmth of his. "Good night, Martin," she whispered a bit tremulously. Pivoting fearfully away, she couldn't bear to have him see the regret shimmering in her eyes.

"Wait...." He took her hand. "Cara. I'm breaking the damned rules, I know. But—" He sighed heavily.

She turned to look back at him.

"What, Martin?" Cara softened in spite of herself. Unable to stop herself, she asked, "What's wrong?"

"Stay with me tonight."

She blinked in stunned surprise as he pulled her close, whispering, "Cara, you want the truth? Well— I want you. I should have my head examined. You're no good for me, and I'm not what you want, but I need you—" his voice quivered, almost breaking, and he paused before he could go on "—to make love to me and mean it. Just once. You can go back to fighting with me tomorrow, but not now. I feel like a damned dead battery." He crushed her to him, tempting her ear with his soft breath, "Don't say no."

His cheek was rough against hers with a day's growth of beard, and there was an odd dampness against her cheek. Tears? She swallowed spasmodically as he held her, not sure if they were hers or his. The world around them was blurry as she felt his heart thudding rapidly against her own. What was he saying? He wanted her, needed her? She could defend against anything but this unexpected, touching candor.

"Cara..." His hard male lips moved across her cheek as he whispered her name, and her breathing became even more ragged and uneven. How was she to say no? How was she to escape such a disarming plea? She fought the stinging in her eyes as a wave of longing and raw hunger swept through her, washing away all her defenses.

"Martin." She reached up, smoothing back his hair. "We are bad for each other."

"I know," he muttered against her lips. "Let me come up."

Closing her eyes, she could only nod, a tight breathlessness in her chest restricting her voice.

"My God," he breathed, his voice a ragged whisper, "is that yes?"

A small shuddering feeling went through her as she lifted her eyes to meet his. "Yes...."

She walked toward her bedroom as though she were in a trance. It was Martin who made sure that the door was locked behind them. His touch had caused a feeling of extreme weakness in her legs, and it was all Cara could do to move in a straight line. She felt like a wanton, with him trailing silently behind her, still holding her hand. Even that small touch filled her with a hungry need, and she quickened her pace, the havoc deep in her core unbelievably intense. Why did his vulnerability make her own fortress so assailable? Why did his openness make her so devastatingly susceptible to his desires? Why was the sight of him, the soft need in his voice, like a blow to her heart?

She couldn't think about it now. All she could do was lead him to her bed and give him what he needed—what she wanted to give. Just this once. He was right. They were bad for each other. Tomorrow they could go back to fighting. Tonight it would be only this one time—one isolated event—meaning nothing.

Her dress floated to the ground at her feet before he lifted her tenderly to the bed, his mouth leaving a trail of fire from her throbbing lips to her aching breasts.

"Cara..." His tormenting, tempting mouth tugged and pulled against her softness, draining her of everything but the delight of being a woman.

She whimpered his name tremulously, wrapping her hands about his head, running her fingers through the soft, straight hair as he drew her breast into his mouth. She dropped her face to his hair, kissing the softness, smelling the woodsy fragrance of after-shave. "Oh, Martin, yes. Yes." Her whole world was concentrated on the wizardry of his tongue, and she felt an urgent quickening of her need for him.

With one last, devastating tug on her breast, spiraling her senses into the realm of total surrender, he lifted his lips. "Damn, Cara," he whispered, his voice hoarse with desire as he pulled her full against his taut body. She opened her eyes to look down at his face. Those eyes, those glorious, bedroom eyes, were glistening with a sensuous fever. "You get to me like no-body I've ever known. I wish—" he whispered urgently, but didn't finish.

"What?" she asked breathlessly.

He shook his head. His lips closed over hers as he murmured, "Nothing... forget it."

Martin Dante proved once again to be anything but conservative in his sexual prowess. In the next hour, Cara forgot that she and Martin were totally wrong for each other, and she didn't care. She only knew that everything he did, every move he made, gave her pleasure in the extreme. His lips were as soft as his moans of pleasure, as he let himself go within their joined passions. And she took as much pleasure in his ecstasy as in her own.

When, at last, they were lying quietly, entwined in the wreckage of the bedding, Cara sighed. It was a contented, purring sound, even in her ears. The arm that he had draped possessively over her flat stomach slid farther about her, hugging her hip intimately to his flat belly. He brushed his lips against her temple. "What are you thinking?"

Closing her eyes, she enjoyed the feel and fragrance of his breath on her face. "I don't want to think." The question she heard herself ask, came out of its own accord. "You?"

His hand missed no curve or valley of her body as it slid up from her waist to stroke her tangled hair. "About you, Cara." The sound of her name when he spoke it sent a shudder of wanting to her core.

"Are you cold?" he asked, mistaking the quiver that he felt in her.

"No." She turned away from him, pressing her back into his inviting warmth. "Anything but cold."

"Everything but." His sigh of contentment sent another shiver of delight through her as he repeated, "Everything."

When he pulled her more snugly against him, she laid her hand across his and smiled serenely, still flushed with the fulfillment of his lovemaking. She caressed his hand with small fluttery strokes, whispering, "Stay with me tonight, Martin."

His only answer was a gentle kiss on her shoulder. She closed her eyes as a warm, new sensation swept over her—an unexpected serenity she had never expected to feel in a man's embrace. This was no trap, it was a haven—a home.

"Martin?" Dawn light filtered through the blinds as Cara turned to put her arms about the man who had filled her dreams with sweetness. She tilted her head back on the pillow so that she could see his face. Somehow, she wasn't surprised to see that he was watching her. A gentle smile lifted his lips. "Yes?" he whispered, his voice endearingly husky with sleep.

"You are going to vote, aren't you?"

She could see his slashing dimple appear as he smiled down at her. "I suppose that question shouldn't surprise me." He bent to kiss her nose. "What would you like for breakfast?"

She twisted around in his arms to face him. "I don't eat breakfast, Martin. Now, I'm serious. Who are you voting for, for governor?"

"No one," he murmured, tightening his arms about her. "Kiss me."

She laughed delightedly, brushing his chin with a finger. It felt rough. "Mmm," she said with a sigh. "Never shave again. I like your chin this way. You feel so—so male."

He grinned devilishly. "You don't." He stroked her bare hip, murmuring in her ear, "Let's make love."

She felt giddy and giggled like a schoolgirl. In a state of happy euphoria, she decided to tease him—play hard to get—just a little. Purposely she slid her hands to his chest and coyly pulled far enough away to get his undivided attention. "No more kissing, Mr. Dante, until you tell me you're a Donnelly Wakefield fan."

His smile faded slightly as a twinge of jealousy smacked him. Choosing to ignore it, he soothed, "Cara, I told you that subject is taboo."

With a playful pout she coaxed him. "Last night we were into trust and truth." She curled a finger in the mat of dark hair on his chest. "Even though it's morning, you can trust me to keep your secret. Tell me you're voting for Donnelly."

He leaned his head back on the pillow and stared up at the ceiling. "I'd rather not talk about Wakefield just now, if you don't mind." It came out in a tired breath.

"But I do, Martin. It's important to me to know." She pulled up and sat on her knees, covering her nudity with the sheet. "You asked me for something last night," she reminded him with a stubborn lift of one brow. Keeping his preference from her now was not

only silly, it was downright insulting. Surely he realized that.

He lowered his gaze to meet hers but said nothing.

Swallowing spasmodically at his close perusal, her
bullheaded determination forced her to blunder on.
"And . . . and I gave you what you needed. Surely you
don't think that was easy for me. I'm not in the
habit—" Once again she couldn't finish. If she weren't
cautious she'd make a terribly stupid and damning
confession, like *I'm just so dangerously drawn to you,
only you, that I don't have the sense or will to say no.*
As she struggled silently for words, his beautiful eyes
became narrowed, guarded.

"Last night wasn't easy for you?" he asked in a
disbelieving whisper. "What you're saying then, is you
let me come up here out of pity?" He stood, facing her
squarely. "I see." He watched her eyes widen. "I've
been a lot of things to a lot of women, but lady—" his
nostrils flared with emotion, yet he kept his voice low
"—I've never been a charity case before." Very fleet-
ingly a bitter smile twisted his lips. "Speaking of pity,"
he said, his silvery eyes cutting into her like steel
blades, "I won't hold you to our little bet, after all.
I've lost my taste for the idea." Dismissing her completely, he turned away.

Why did he have to look so gloriously male and be
so unnervingly magnetic as he pulled on his clothes?
It made her furious to be so attracted to him. Driven
by demons dredged up in her emotional upheaval, she
shot defensively, "Don't pity *me*, Mr. Dante. Worry
about yourself! Lucy told me everybody at the club

heard us yelling. They're all making bets on us. So it's too late for *you* to weasel out.''

He had turned back and was standing indolently now, his shirt open, his eyes mere specks of sparking silver beneath lowered brows. ''Heard?'' With a scornful smile tugging at one corner of his mouth, he asked, ''I don't mind for myself, but aren't you concerned for your reputation?''

Smarting over the irritatingly impersonal timbre of his voice, she shook her head and worked to sound equally cool, though she had to fight an overwhelming urge to cry. ''They think I'm going to cook you dinner. Nobody knows about—the other.''

''For once, a reputation is saved by misinformation,'' he returned evenly. ''At least you'll have that to cling to.'' He pivoted away in that precise yet graceful way he had, and was gone. Before she could move or react, she heard the front door open and then close quietly, too quietly. She would have slammed his door so hard it would have brought down light fixtures!

With a sob, feeling empty and lost, she threw herself onto the rumpled bed. She was horrified to discover that she was in love with Martin Dante, and he didn't even care enough to slam her door!

Chapter Ten

Curiosity killed the cat, Cara," she muttered to herself as she slammed the door of her Pinto. "Isn't there any way I can talk you out of this?" Her hand bullied its way past her good sense to the ignition and jammed the key in. The motor chugged to a start as she caught a glimpse of hazel eyes in the rearview mirror. They were stubborn eyes, narrowed in grim determination. "Fool," she sputtered, as she backed out of her parking space.

That was the end of her mumbled conversation. She was no longer on speaking terms with herself. Jaws clamped shut, she doggedly headed toward the South Regional Library, Tulsa's newest, a sleek, low glass structure in one of the building complexes that surrounded Oklahoma's largest indoor shopping mall,

Woodland Hills. Martin was scheduled to be the speaker at the first of several Tulsa Run clinics designed to prepare jogging enthusiasts for the October twenty-eighth event.

She bit the same place on the inside of her cheek that she'd bitten that morning when she'd seen his disgustingly handsome face smiling up from above the headline, Computer Data Prez Sees Lighter Side of Life on Jogging Trail. The article went on to explain that Martin Dante's talk would be a "lesson in levity, tempting runners to loosen up and laugh at themselves."

"Ha!" she snapped, swerving around a corner, tires squealing. "Since when has that man ever laughed at himself!" This she had to see.

It wasn't a bright thing to do. She should be at home right now sticking mailing labels on campaign material, making calls for donations, or for that matter, sleeping. But no, she was running around town to hear Martin Dante speak. And why?

Because she was a fool! That was why, plain and simple. She hadn't seen him in a month. Well, that wasn't totally accurate. She'd seen him. Once, he'd been leaving for work when she'd gone out to get her paper. It had been early, not quite seven in the morning, but there he was.

She had been in her flannel robe and fluffy slippers. Her hair still looked as if it'd been slept in. True to gentlemanly tradition, he'd scooped up her paper and handed it to her, filling her head with his scent. He hadn't smiled. But the eye contact, though fleeting, had been memorable and debilitating. She'd stood there, her paper clutched in her arms, watching as he ducked into his car. Mercifully she had been able to force her limbs to turn away before he switched on his engine and she was gone by the time he backed out.

She'd seen him three times since then. But of course she wasn't counting. All three times, he had come home with a woman. First it had been Jane, the other times it had been the girl from the park. As Cara turned into the library parking lot, her lips lifted in a self-deprecating smile. All three times she'd seen him with women, he'd seen her with groceries. She doubted if he ever wondered about her, but if he did, he must figure she was totally into food. She chuckled as she stepped from the car, but she didn't feel happy.

"Cara!"

She turned to see Donnelly Wakefield waving broadly to attract her attention. He stood between her and the glass-and-steel library, which was so bright with the fiery reflection of a red sunset that she had to squint to make out his lean silhouette as he angled back toward her.

Donnelly called, "I thought that was your car. You coming to scout the competition?"

Cara winced. By now, most of her friends had heard about the bet. She shrugged, zipping the front of her yellow velour warm-up and plunging her hands into her pockets. "I could ask you the same question," she parried. "I didn't know you were going to run, Donnelly."

He shook his head. "I'm not. I, like you, I imagine, am curious about what Martin will say. He seems like a nice guy." Donnelly slid a hand to her elbow. "I hope I can get to know him better after the election. He's one hell of a bright man."

Cara pursed her lips without answering, and they entered the building in silence, turning left toward the large conference room.

"Say, there's Martin at the door." Before Cara could think of any reasonable objection, Donnelly hailed him, calling over the heads of a steady flow of people. "Hello, Martin." With Cara in tow, he stopped by the entrance where Martin had been talking to a cluster of people. When he turned toward them, his face registered brief surprise before easing into a cordial half smile that didn't reach his eyes. Once again she regretted her trek over here. She'd planned on sneaking in and out without Martin ever knowing that she'd attended the talk. She now felt uncomfortable under his guarded scrutiny, and wondered what hateful thoughts were running through his mind.

Her lashes fluttered and dropped as she swung her gaze away from his lips. She tried to look at something else, anything else, but failed. The big, plain-walled room held no interest. Almost immediately her eyes were pulled back to his as though by a magnet.

"Hello," Martin addressed them both, but he was watching her. "I didn't expect to see either of you here."

Cara braced for battle, remarking brittlely, "I had to see this—Martin Dante giving a speech on how to laugh at himself. I can't imagine you pulling enough stuffing out of your shirt to do this."

His gaze was level and intense and he didn't answer immediately. "I had some help," he remarked finally, apparently not intending to elaborate.

She stared at him, her mind fumbling at what he might mean by that. His eyes were quietly probing, making her uncomfortable. She dropped her gaze to his throat.

Donnelly filled the tense breach. "Well, I'm looking forward to this, Dante." He reached out to shake Martin's hand. "Of course, your competitor here is, too, no matter what she says." He indicated Cara with a teasing grin.

"Competitor?" Martin shook Donnelly's hand, but didn't move his eyes from Cara. "Are you still planning to run?"

"Of course." She glanced back up at him, jutting a stubborn chin. "Why do you keep asking me that question?"

Martin slid his gaze from her to Donnelly and back to her. With a slight shrug, he said, "No reason. I just thought..." He let the sentence drop. Then he indicated a long bank of tables at the back of the room. There were several lines of people waiting by them. "If you really plan to run, you can sign up tonight and get your Run packet and registration number. Or you can wait. There's still time to change your mind."

"I'm not changing my mind, Martin. A bet is a bet." Deep down, she wished for some graceful way to back out of this thing—a broken leg would be nice. But everybody in the world was betting on them. She'd never live it down if she quit now. With all the heartiness she could muster she affirmed, "No reason to wait. I'll sign up tonight."

"Fine." He accepted her declaration simply. Shifting to look more directly toward Donnelly, he asked, "And you're running, too?"

Donnelly's laughter was deep. "Only for governor. The evening of the run I'm debating Andrew Mathison. I figure I'd better save my energy for that."

Cara thought she saw Martin's brow crease in a slight frown. The impression was brief, but she was sure that it had been there. No doubt Martin was uncomfortable about discussing the election—especially with one of the candidates. His next question made her start. "I'm curious, Donnelly, how do you feel about our... bet?"

Donnelly's smile grew wide and he shook his head as though in disbelief. "Ah, the bet." He claimed Cara's elbow. "I'm afraid I have no choice but to go with Cara. She's been too loyal to desert in her hour of trial." He passed Cara a brief wink as he went on. "For as long as I've known her, I've never seen her fail at anything she's really wanted to do. So, I wish you luck, Martin."

Martin lifted a brow. "Hmm." He dropped his gaze to Cara, looking doubtful. "Maybe you should be giving this talk." He held out a hand. "Wish me luck?" She made no move to lift her hand from her side, but neither did she work at avoiding him. Somehow it didn't surprise her that he took her hand, anyway. His grip was warm and steady.

"You? Luck!" Cara blinked, feeling uneasy under his close, silver scrutiny, and highly irritated that her senses were much too aware of his touch. Pulling her hand from his, she leveled sparking, hazel eyes at him and took a defensive shot. "Did the North wish the South luck?"

He lifted his cast-off hand, crossing his arms before his sleek, black warm-up jacket. Cara tried not to notice that it was only zipped a third of the way up. Underneath the jacket he was wearing a matching nylon jogging T-shirt that did little to disguise the muscled chest or the wiry mat of black hair that spilled over the scooped-out neck. She watched the broad chest expand as he inhaled, explaining. "I meant, would you wish me luck for tonight?"

After a painfully extended silence, Donnelly squeezed Cara's elbow. Had it been a cattle prod, she would have been propelled into Martin's chest. Anticipating correctly that her silence was not about to come to an end, he filled the tense gap. "Of course we do, Martin. Good luck."

One brow lifted slightly as Martin's eyes slid from Cara's face to Donnelly's and then back to Cara. "Thanks." His expression was pleasant enough, but there was no humor in his eyes. "By the way, Dennis tells me your students have had good results with our Fit-Calc program."

His continued nearness and the abrupt subject change rattled Cara. She cleared her throat nervously. "Oh—that." Stalling for time, she tossed her head in a gesture that she hoped appeared careless. What could she say? The nutritional program had been a godsend to a number of her students. Many of them who had been frustrated by failures with fad diets were finally losing weight and eating well-balanced meals, too. They praised Martin and his program at every class. It would have been only fair to tell him so. But his rejection still stung more painfully than she cared to admit.

Unable to look him directly in the eye, she gazed aimlessly about the room. In a monotone, she mumbled, "Some of the women are enthusiastic, I suppose." Her eyes flitted back to his and wouldn't be separated. Her heart began to hammer at his unwavering watchfulness. Those eyes, so deceptively sleepy, so bewitching. She could feel herself weakening under the sorcery of his male allure and felt an overwhelming urge to be taken into his arms, to feel again the serenity she had known there.

But there was no *true* serenity with a man. It was all a sham—Martin was a bedeviling sham, she had to admit—but a trap, nevertheless. She didn't like or respect him, and planned to put a stop to her problem this instant by pushing him so far away that he would never want to be close to her again.

Steeling herself for the fray, she prepared to fire a protective volley. Boldly, she lifted her chin and predicted, "Don't fret, Martin. Fit-Calc will probably make you a million dollars. I know that's what's important to you—sitting on your safe little fence and making tons of money."

Her remark left both men speechless and staring. Martin waited almost a full minute before he spoke, all the while studying her rigid face. "Thanks, Professor," he murmured as his mouth twitched in a wry half smile. "That's a great weight off my mind."

Turning toward Donnelly he nodded. "If you'll excuse me, I'd better get ready."

When he had walked a few paces away, Donnelly bent down near Cara's ear and spoke in a low whisper. "Did your daddy ever paddle you?"

"No." For some demented reason, she couldn't drag her eyes from Martin's retreating figure. "My parents didn't believe in physical punishment. Why?"

Donnelly's finger on her chin drew her reluctant gaze to meet his skeptical expression. "It's too bad, my little dove, that you didn't inherit your parents' nonviolent ways."

"What do you mean, Donnelly?" She frowned up at him. "I didn't hit the man."

He smiled sadly at her and shook his head. "Are you quite sure?"

Cara's eyes sparkled with defiance but she didn't want to fight with him. And though she wouldn't have admitted it, even to herself, she felt a little guilty about what she'd said to Martin. No matter how she tried, she couldn't erase the memory of the strange shadows she'd seen flicker across his eyes. It had seemed, as Donnelly had said, almost as though she'd struck him with her words.

She'd wanted to put distance between them, and it looked as though she had. Somehow, it didn't make her feel particularly victorious. With a long sigh, she shrugged. "Why don't you go find us some seats while I get signed up for this little jog?"

"Look for me near the back. I have a meeting at eight, so I may have to slip out."

Clutching her Tulsa Run Kit, Cara shifted in her molded chair. It was comfortable enough, but she was not. With each burst of laughter from the audience, she sank lower in her seat, wishing she were dead. The president of the Tulsa Runners' Club had introduced Martin and listed his credits. She'd known most of them through articles she'd read about him over the years. But one thing that she had neglected to glean anywhere was an unpalatable bit of information about how Martin had just missed qualifying to run in the Olympics when he was in college.

Well, one thing was sure, he was much older now. Still, she felt a vague unease in the pit of her stomach. He was going to be pretty fair competition for her—to put it mildly. As a matter of fact, there was a nasty little voice buzzing in her ear like a gnat that kept suggesting that if she bet the right money on Martin, she could get that antique dining room table she'd been wanting. Her short nails raked the large packet in her lap. It held her Tulsa Run shirt, headband and contestant number. She hadn't looked through everything, but she was pretty sure it also held her Waterloo. In her case the Waterloo was twenty-four hours of cooking and 'catering' for Martin Dante. With a grimace, she sank even lower.

Another laugh went up among the spectators, and Cara's eyes flitted back up to Martin. He no longer wore the warm-up suit.

Now, he was clad only in the sleeveless tank top, black nylon shorts and jogging shoes. Damn him, anyway! Why did he have to look like a model up

there? And by the smiling faces around her, he was
apparently being quite witty, too.

People were giggling, and Cara was chewing her lip
when Donnelly nudged her. "It's almost eight, Cara.
I've got to go. Tell Martin I enjoyed his talk."

She cocked her head sideways to toss him a grim
frown. "Sure."

His wry grin told her that he didn't believe that for
one minute. "Never mind. I'll tell him later."

When her eyes returned to Martin, he was grinning
in her direction. "And finally, one important thing
that I think is never stressed enough." He'd been
leaning a muscular hip against a table. As he shifted
away from it, Cara watched the powerful muscles on
his thighs flex with the movement. "Always keep a
wary eye out for stationary objects; if you don't,
somewhere out there a tree—or a wall—has your name
on it."

She stared at him, feeling the needle in his remark
as the oblivious audience applauded. He had meant
that for her! Stationary objects—a wall! She ground
her teeth, hoping that there would be time for rebut-
tals.

Straightening from her hunched position, she
looked around. Martin had been engulfed by a crowd
of well-wishers. Good. Though she didn't expect him
to seek her out to taunt her any further personally, his
imprisonment among the many would give her a
chance to escape. She got caught in the press of milling, laughing people, and chafed inwardly at the de-
lay in getting to the door.

Finally, she took matters into her own hands. "Excuse me." Using her packet like a wedge, she angled her way through tight little groups of slender, tanned people. She was used to slender people, but not to so many so tightly packed. "Pardon—uh—" She closed one eye, wincing with the pain as a big boot found her foot and flattened it.

She pulled her lips between her teeth. It was a pitiful excuse for a brave smile, but it was the best she could do. Looking up at a tall cowboy, she assured him weakly, "That's okay...no, no, I'm fine, really." She had to alternate from a nod that she was fine, to a refusing shake of her head at his insistence that he buy her a drink, or coffee or dinner, as she struggled through the exit. She continued to fend off the persistent young man, declaring, "Limping? Heavens no, I'm not limping, I always walk this way. Comes from living on the side of a hill." Avoiding the cowboy's gape-jawed expression, she pivoted away, and as quickly as she could, impeded as she was, Cara headed for her car.

She'd unlocked it, pulled the door open and was about to duck inside, when she was restrained by a hand on her shoulder. "Okay. Take a look at my nose and tell me what you see." She'd stiffened, fearing that it was the cowboy, but the voice was much more familiar than that.

With a foot poised on the frame of the car, she peered sideways to look at the long fingers that were restraining her. Then, slowly, she stepped down and turned to face him. "Fishing for compliments, Martin? What's wrong? Did your groupies in there forget to praise your nose when they were showering you with flattery?"

That drew a crooked smile from him, and he moved his hand from her shoulder and rested it on the top of her car, leaning over her slightly. "I see you've overcome your urge to be pleasant again."

She averted her head, scanning the sky above his shoulder. It was black velvet, sprinkled with diamond dust. "Your nose works passably well with the rest of your face, Martin. Now will that be all?"

"My nose is perfect, Cara."

She sniffed, turning back to look at his face. "You don't need me, Martin. You're very good at flattering yourself."

He tapped the end of the bodily part being discussed. "No. I mean, it's not broken. When I saw you and Donnelly come in tonight, I thought that was why you were here. So that Donnelly could break my nose."

She crossed her arms before her and stared up at him. "Well, if he didn't already have it, that'd assure him my vote, but I can't see much reason for his breaking your nose otherwise. What are you talking about?"

His gaze gleamed with a silvery intensity, difficult to hold and impossible to break away from. "Just that, if I were seeing a woman, I would break any man's nose who made a bet with her like the one I made with you. Donnelly says he knows about the bet. But just what does he think you're going to do for me for twenty-four hours if you lose?"

"He knows exactly what I told Lucy; if I, by some freak happenstance, don't beat you, I cook and cater to you—for a day," she gritted. "Of course, their definition of 'cater'—as well as mine—is not so far-reaching as yours. They think I'll be cooking for you—maybe do a little scrubbing. They also think it's quite funny. You see, it's fairly widely known that I don't cook very well, and that I believe men can scrub as well as women!"

"I see." He put his other palm on the top of her car, forcing her to back into the cold metal or be uncomfortably close to his lips. Even so, her head and shoulders were still trapped between his arms. "Are you, or are you not, seeing Donnelly?" His soft question startled her with its bluntness.

"Seeing Donnelly? Of course, I'm seeing Donnelly. I see him several times a week at a function or meeting—"

He shook his head, cutting her short. "No. By seeing, I mean involved. Are you involved with Donnelly?" His piercing question sliced through her pretense of normality.

Her throat felt dry, and her cheeks burned as she quickly tore her eyes away from him. "I . . . I'm devoted to Donnelly."

"Not good enough."

When she turned back, which she couldn't seem to help doing, he tipped his head to the side, indulgently curious. "Well?" There was a warm, intimate quality in the low-toned question.

She swallowed, wishing this conversation were not taking place. "Martin," she squeaked. Stopping to clear her throat, she went on. "I'm not involved with Donnelly. I'm not involved with anyone. That's the way I want it."

"Why?"

The lights spilling from the library entry made his silver streak wink brightly in the darkness of his hair. She fought a dangerous softening and glared up at him. "Because men keep wanting to *change* me."

"I can't imagine why." With the teasing gleam in his eye, Cara couldn't tell if he'd complimented or insulted her. She lifted a warning finger. "Now don't get any ideas, Martin. I swore off men over two years ago. I like what I do, and I like how I do it. I'm thirty-four, and I'm not going to change my life just to have a man."

"Not even Donnelly?" he mocked, devilish lights dancing in his light eyes.

"Not even *you*!" she countered in a burst of impatience, and then bit down hard on her tongue when she realized what she had admitted.

There was a glimmer of surprise in his look. "Me?" he asked with a curious inclination of his head. "I was under the impression you hated my guts."

"Martin...I..." she stammered, thrashing around for a way to save herself. He managed to thwart her so well with small, verbal weapons that she had given him. What hell could he put her through if he knew that she was helplessly attracted to him? "I didn't mean that the way it sounded." Licking dry lips, she leaped wildly to another subject, trying to put him on the defensive. "And...and anyway, why didn't you tell me you'd almost qualified to run in the Olym-

pics? I have a half a mind to . . . to back out of the bet
now. You *hustled* me!" Feeling frustrated to the limit
of her wits, she pushed out on his elbows. "Back off,
will you? You're giving me claustrophobia."

He obliged her with only one of his arms. The other
he left planted on the top of her car. It grazed her
shoulder, shouting its heated presence with every pulsating second. His gaze was far from lazy as his eyes
worked to penetrate her brain. She tried to think about
nothing, fearing that he might be able to read her telling thoughts.

When he spoke, he spoke quietly. "I didn't hustle
you and you know it. And why would I tell anyone I
almost qualified for the Olympics? That's like saying
you're almost normal. No one brags about almosts.
The guy who introduced me must have gone behind
my back and called my mother. Isobel would be the
only person to remember that."

"Don't try to shove this off on your mother! I say
you hustled me, and I think I'll just back out of this
bet. You could have warned me."

"I told you I was good."

Sarcasm lifted her lips. "Sure, and Barbra Strei-
sand sings a little."

His nostrils flared, and his expression didn't regis-
ter any humor. "No, Cara. Not now. The bet stands.
Unlike Dante Alighieri, I do not intend to let my Beatrice walk away without a fight."

Cara knew that he was referring to the woman
whom the epic poet who bore Martin's last name had
loved from afar. Dante had made Beatrice immortal
in his *Divine Comedy*. In it Beatrice leads Dante

through the joys of heaven after he has made a trip through the Inferno. Recalling what was written over the gate of hell in Dante's poem, she lifted her chin, quoting in a sardonic growl, "All hope abandon, ye who enter here." With a toss of her head, she added a challenging quip. "Because I'm going to beat the pants off you!"

He slid his hand from the car's surface to the nape of her neck. "There's an easier way to get my pants off, Cara."

She didn't know if it was the cool caress of his fingers, or the casual assurance of his suggestive statement that sent the shiver up her spine. Twisting her head, she drew away from his touch and dived into the car. Blood pounded in her ears as she gripped the steering wheel. Between clenched teeth, she spit out, "I know. Spill red wine on them!" Refusing to look back up into those eyes, she snapped, "Would you mind closing the door? I'm getting chilled."

"Not at all." She could barely hear the padding sound of his jogging shoes as he stepped away. "We wouldn't want you to catch cold, now would we?" The door clicked shut at her side. Her body remained rigid, facing forward, but her eyes followed Martin's casual retreat in the side-view mirror, his short-clad form silhouetted in the golden light that reached out from the library and embraced his contours.

He was such a fantastic-looking animal—tall and lean, with trim hips that pressed seductively against the brief shorts as he walked. She wondered if he had any idea how flagrantly the sight of his slightly rounded derriere in action affected her?

With her knuckles turning white in her death grip on the wheel, she let out a long, low breath. Martin Dante could beat her. He could beat her physically, and if she wasn't terribly careful he could break her emotionally, too. He was the one man left in the world who had the power. She was a gazelle in the wild, running free, living by her wits and whims and hurting no one. She could run long and hard, but it was now becoming distressingly clear that he could run longer and harder. Her throat closed with the very real fear that she could end up crushed.

Chapter Eleven

Cara had been prepared to ignore Martin with all her energies, ready to avoid him at all costs, and mentally armed to rebuff him with pithy and sage rhetoric, before tossing a defiant head and walking triumphantly away. The only thing she had not prepared for in all her cold-shouldering rehearsals was for Martin to be gone.

But he was. Martin Dante was just no longer there. He still lived below her, but in the past month before the election, Martin had been dividing his time between Wakefield's Tulsa headquarters and Mathison's Oklahoma City offices. And if he wasn't out of town, his car rumbled in so late that she would have had to rush outside in her nightgown to exhibit her haughty disinterest in him. Somehow, having to go to such lengths to show someone that you didn't care if he lived or died made the ostracism lose its bite. So she just didn't see him.

Besides, she had been busy, too, with her sociology classes, self-discovery seminars, aerobics and volunteer work for Donnelly's campaign. She was feeling a little down right now. It was probably because she was tired, but at the moment, even the steps to her home seemed almost too high to climb.

Donnelly was running behind Mathison in the latest polls, and that was depressing, too. But Raleigh was hopeful that his popularity hadn't peaked yet. There were still indications that Donnelly was gaining a stronger backing in these final days. But win or lose, right now Cara had to admit that she would be glad to see the flurry of election preparations grind to an end. The rub was that to get there, she had to make it through the Tulsa Run—tomorrow.

Heaving a sigh, she trudged up the steps and fumbled in her bag for her key. Tomorrow. The key turned easily and she pushed into the shadowed entry. It was only five o'clock, but the trees shaded the building so well that it was excessively dark inside. Flipping on a light, she crossed to the kitchen, wondering what she had the energy to fix for dinner—tap water came to mind, and she heaved another sigh.

The light that filtered in from the living area fell on a notepad, propped up on the counter. A frown of curiosity creased her forehead as she lifted it. It was in Raleigh's fine hand.

"Hi, Champ. Look in your refrig. Evan whipped
you up a private little 'carbo' dinner to help you
speed through the run tomorrow. Martin mentioned that there would be a big lasagna feast
down at the Williams Center Forum tonight for
any runner who wanted to come. Said there'd be
nearly five thousand people there. He asked if
you were coming. I said I doubted it. Anyway,
Evan wanted to do this, and I think it was a nice
idea. There's one light beer in the frig, too. I
know you don't like beer, but force some. Think
of it as carbohydrate fuel!

                                    Love, Ral

There was a P.S.: Oh, sorry we won't be there to
cheer you on, but Donnelly is taping that debate in
OKC, so we'll be out of town. But our hearts will be
with your feet!

Cara's lips quivered in a grateful smile as she
dropped the notepad to the counter and went to the
refrigerator to find Evan's gift. It was a huge pan. She
and at least one hundred of the eleven-odd thousand
people who were expected to run tomorrow could have
shared it with her. She pulled it out of the refrigerator
and put it in the oven, silently thanking Evan for his
thoughtfulness. Switching on the oven, she inhaled,
her depression lifting measurably. It would be at least
forty-five minutes before the food heated up. Outside, the weather was lovely and mild for late October. When was the last time she'd had a minute to
really enjoy a colorful autumn day? Not this year.

She'd never even walked in the woods behind the condominium. How many times had she promised herself to do that?

Hunter's Pointe, the palatial housing development where Martin was building his house, was just a couple of blocks back through the trees. It would be fun to wander around the quiet, well-manicured homes that surrounded two sparkling ponds.

Ten minutes later, she'd changed into jeans and a multicolored chenille jacket. Zipping it up, she recalled how Evan had teased her about it, asking her if she'd defaced some poor old granny's bedspread to get it. The thought made her smile. Evan had been a real shot in the arm for her family.

She locked her door behind her and galloped down the steps two at a time. Inhaling the brisk, nutty fall air, she circled around to the back of her condo and headed into the trees. Minutes later, she was ambling along the narrow private road that meandered up and down the hilly landscape of Hunter's Pointe. Hands thrust into her jacket pockets, she smiled at the peaceful sight of a family of geese as they skimmed the surface of the smaller of Hunter's Pointe's two ponds. She crossed a bridge, and headed up a gradual incline that would take her around a bend to another pond. Halfway there, her eye was caught by new construction. That wasn't unusual, she'd already seen several new homes in various stages of completion, but this one held her interest. It was nearly five-thirty now, and the workers would be gone, so Cara stepped off onto the newly graded yard to take a closer look.

The house, built on a lot that sloped toward the pond, was contemporary, yet borrowed freely from the past. It was constructed of redwood and street paving bricks rescued from Tulsa's urban renewal. It was set back from the curving road among autumn-tinted oaks and yellow-leafed hickory trees. The massive structure was two stories high, with three gabled sections nestled into the hillside.

The circular driveway had been poured, and Cara walked across the pebbled surface heading around the side of the house on a path of pavers set in an intricate design. In the rear, the path turned into a courtyard that surrounded a pool. A wide fan of steps led up to a partially constructed deck, where a wall of long windows and double doors dominated, providing gracious access to the pool. On the far side of the pool area there was another, smaller building in the process of being finished. Cara guessed that it would be used as a bathhouse for visitors who wanted to shower and change after a swim.

She stepped over the frame of the deck and picked her way through builders' debris to peek at the interior. The ceilings were high and the trim was rich. A parquet floor was in the process of being stained. Cara squinted to see beyond in the fading light. A fireplace dominated the far end of the room, banked on either side by walls of shelves. Cara pressed her lips together in awe. Even from this distance, she could tell that someone had gone to a good deal of trouble to have the antique marble mantel installed. Whoever was building this house was sparing no expense to have the best.

She picked her way over the uneven ground that would one day be a deck, then stopped at a long window and peered inside. It was the kitchen, with a high sloping ceiling and exposed beams. Skylights along one wall gave the room a bright, open feeling. It was lovely—even to someone who considered a kitchen an unnatural part of a home.

A breeze filtered cold air through her light jacket, and Cara shivered. It was nearly six, and the temperature was dropping with the sun. Regretting that she was unable to see any more of the inside, she hugged her arms beneath her breasts, and headed back toward the front of the house.

When she rounded the corner, she smashed headlong into a human wall. "Oh!" she gasped, throwing her arms out protectively.

"Oof," was the answer that came back, as something warm and strong grabbed her waist, halting her backward stumble.

It didn't take a genius to know that she'd run into someone. Probably the builder, or worse, the owner of the house, and she immediately began to apologize for trespassing. "I . . . I'm sorry, I was just taking a walk. . . ."

The smile that met her stuttering explanation paralyzed her lips, and she forgot what she had been about to say. She breathed a disbelieving moan with his name. "Martin?"

He didn't let go of her. "Are you all right?"

She stared up at his handsome, aggressively male face. A distant part of her mind registered the fact that the white dress shirt was open at the neck. Working hard to ignore the sensuous attraction he exuded, she ran a hand self-consciously through her hair, unable to come up with even one of the pithy rebuffs she had rehearsed so diligently. Where was her mind? Without a clue about what she was going to say, she mumbled, "Uh...I'm a little dizzy, I guess."

His hands slid out to her arms, as his eyes covered her slender form with a thorough appraisal. "Good. That's normal for you." Before she had time to realize just what he had said and retort with appropriate effrontery, he released one of her arms and turned away. Lifting a hand, he acknowledged a newcomer, a handsome, ash-blond woman in her late fifties. Wearing an excellently tailored mauve silk suit, she stood quietly behind him, her expression closed in a worried frown. "Mother, I'd like you to meet one of my condominium neighbors, Cara Torrence."

The well-preserved face opened in mild surprise, banishing the worry. Then, with a prim poise, she unclasped her hands and held one out. "Miss Torrence? If memory serves, I believe Martin has mentioned you."

Now it was Cara's turn to express surprise. But as quickly as she took Mrs. Dante's offered hand, she regained her control. Still feeling the sting of Martin's earlier cut, she smiled sweetly. "Oh? Did he tell you that I intend to beat him in the Tulsa Run tomorrow?"

"No." Both women looked up as Martin answered. Dropping their hands, they waited for him to go on. He drew his mother under a protective arm. "What I said, was that 'Cara Torrence gives a whole new meaning to the expression, 'four-letter word.'"" He was watching Cara, and his smile was crooked, teasing. Somehow rather than making Cara angry, it made her eyes sparkle with fun.

Isobel reached up and playfully hit the hand that cupped her shoulder. "Martin! That was certainly not what you said." With an apologetic smile to Cara she lifted a finger to her lips. "Really, Martin, help me out here."

He squeezed her shoulders, passing her a grin. "The apothecary chest."

Isobel clapped her hands together. "That's it. You have a lovely antique one. Martin told me about yours. I love antiques, and my son loves to tease me about finds I've managed to miss."

"Oh." Cara nodded. She was smiling, but there was a stab of regret in the pit of her stomach when she realized that Isobel Dante had heard of her only as an "apothecary chest." How crazy of her to feel disappointed about that. "Yes, I do consider myself lucky about getting it."

"You are, my dear. I'd love to see it sometime." Her hands returned to their clasped position, her smile blossomed and Cara was struck by the woman's youthful beauty. "I'm impressed to find a young person these days with a love for antiques." She lifted a playfully admonishing frown toward her son. "I don't know what I've done wrong." She waved a broad hand toward the massive home under construction. "I can't even get him to build a decent house. Just look at this wildly contemporary thing."

Cara started, her eyes flying to Martin. He snagged the look and held it. "You? Your house?" Her voice was a high-pitched whisper.

He nodded. "Like it?"

Isobel interjected. "Well, of course she'll say she does, Martin. That would only be polite."

His mother looked puzzled when he burst out laughing, but she went on, speaking to Cara. "Actually, I wanted him to buy one of the fine old homes near where I live. Or if he had to build way out here, at least pick something more traditional, like English Georgian. But this!"

"Oh, no." Cara disagreed, turning to look up at it. "It's a lot like him—solidly conservative, but with a flair for the innovative. I think it's perfect."

A rich chuckle at her back made her turn abruptly. She'd complimented him! Defended him against his own mother. She couldn't meet his eyes, couldn't even turn directly toward him. With a quick decision, she again thrust out her hand toward Mrs. Dante, who was smiling a very odd smile. "I...I just remembered, I've got to get back...a date," she lied.

Isobel took her hand again, this time a little more firmly. "Oh? Well, I'm glad to have met you—Cara."

"A date?" Martin was forcing her to look up at him with the darkly skeptical tone in his voice.

Deciding to bluff it through, she lifted a proud chin that dared him to doubt her. "Yes, why?"

He lifted a shoulder in seeming disinterest. "Oh, I just thought you'd want to get plenty of rest tonight. You're going to have a long day tomorrow." His eyes were telling her that there would also be a long night connected to that day.

She troubled the inside of her lip. "Well, aren't you going down to the carbo dinner?"

He shook his head. "Nope. Mother bribed Phillip to cook spaghetti for me tonight. It's become a tradition."

"Bribed?" She was curious, and couldn't help asking.

"Yes, my dear," Isobel answered. "Phillip is my chef. He never cooks anything but French food anymore. But, for a while, he was forced to cook in an Italian restaurant. That's where Martin found him. So every year before the run, we suffer through a small tantrum and offer Phillip two weeks in France to bring back new gourmet recipes, and he relents."

Cara's jaw dropped. "You do all that for spaghetti?"

Martin grinned at her. "You can say that only because you've never eaten Phillip's spaghetti. Why don't you join us?"

She closed her mouth, swallowing. "Uh . . . no. Remember, I'm busy tonight."

"Oh, yes." Martin ran a fist along his chin, his brows inching into a small frown. "Well, try to get to bed—" Beneath languid lids she could see his silvery

gaze shift quickly from her face to his mother's profile and then back to her. After the minute pause, he
amended, "—get home early."

"Yes, Daddy," Cara agreed with a trace of dry-
ness. Turning once more to his mother, she nodded,
smiling stiffly. "Goodbye, Mrs. Dante."

"Please, call me Isobel." She had lifted her hand
back to Martin's, still on her shoulder. Her smile was
kind and open. "I do wish you luck in the run tomorrow. But I must warn you my son is very good."

Martin raised a brow, but said nothing.

Cara pursed her lips, lifting her head in a half nod.
"Yes, he told me. Well, goodbye." Pivoting away, she
began the trek back through the woods. As she
trudged farther and farther away from the sound of
their voices, she berated herself for not having done
this about ten minutes earlier.

Cara wasn't the only person to arrive bright and
early at the downtown Tulsa Williams Center Green.
Thousands of spectators and participants were milling around on a meticulously landscaped central
garden area, complete with bronze statues and
meandering waterspills. It was an exceptionally mild
day for late October, so Cara hadn't worn a warm-up.
She was comfortable in her red nylon hurdler shorts
and a light blue cotton T-shirt that read "I Love
Rhythmic Aerobics" across the front. The word
"love" had been replaced by a red heart that was
strategically located over the left breast—a symbolic

representation of the most important muscle of the body that aerobic exercise benefits.

Cara had never been to the Tulsa Run before, she'd only read about it. Yet even in her overwrought state, she had to admit that being here was quite an experience. A band from Oral Roberts University was playing some upbeat marching music under a brightly striped canopy. Families of some of the runners were scattered about the lawn on blankets or deck chairs with picnic baskets and coolers. Cara laughed to see some of the costumed runners who were here for the two-mile Fun Run. There was everything from a caped and masked costume of Captain Beer Suds to a female runner in pink with her dog in a leash, also wearing pink running shorts and shirt. There were mothers who would be pushing strollers in the race, and daddies pulling wagons. Anything that was fun was fine for the Fun Run.

Serious runners were doing warm-up exercises and discussing race strategy. Cara clenched her jaw in determination. Her only strategy was to beat Martin Dante or die en route—probably on the Hill. That was the nickname used by veteran runners for the last grueling mile of the nine-and-three-tenths-mile race. She'd heard more than one story of runners who ended up staggering and falling on their faces just before making the finish line. She'd seen pictures in the paper of previous races with people being carried off on stretchers. Cara nervously licked her lips. That kind of morbid thinking would do her no good.

She looked at her watch. It was eight-thirty. The run would start in thirty minutes. As she began to stretch out, her mind went back to earlier this morning. Martin had met her by her car and offered her a ride. She'd refused. But he had insisted that she meet him on the steps west of the Performing Arts Center so that they could begin the race together. She didn't want to do that, but she supposed it was the only way to make sure she stayed ahead of him.

After about five good minutes of stretching, she found a drinking fountain and took one last swallow of water. Then she picked her way through feet and legs to find an empty spot on the brick stairway. There were at least two hundred other people on those steps. She smiled inwardly. Maybe he wouldn't find her.

"Cara!" Her expression clouded in a worried frown. Had she heard someone call her name?

"Cara! Cara Torrence! Down here!"

She followed the sound of the voice to a lanky man in cowboy boots. He was waving a Stetson at her and smiling. His jeans were dark blue and held a rich crease, and his western shirt was not the sort of shirt that was designed for work. This was an urban cowboy, if she'd ever seen one. He was motioning for her to come down. Obviously he had a message for her. Maybe luck was with her and he'd come to say that Martin had chickened out. Deep down, she doubted that, but she pushed herself up and picked her way down to the sidewalk. "I'm Cara Torrence. What is it?"

His laugh was light as he put a hand on her elbow and began to maneuver her away from the steps. "I know who ya are, ma'am."

She lifted her elbow out of his grasp, granting him a pointed look of suspicion. "Well, you're one up on me. Would you mind telling me who you are?"

He settled the hat on his head. "Sure. I'm a friend of Martin Dante's. The name's Dunlap. Bobby Dunlap. I'm a member at the Tulsa Racquetball and Aerobics Club. Thought he might have mentioned me to you."

She shook her head. "No. sorry. Do you have a message from Martin?"

"Not exactly. But Martin's why I'm here." He cocked his head away from the steps. "Say, could we move on a little? I don't want him to see us together."

She darted him a curious glance. "Why? You two going steady?"

He shook his head, chuckling. "Mind if we mosey?"

Cara shrugged her assent. "Okay. I have a few minutes. What is it you don't want Martin to see?"

Pulling a pack of cigarettes from his shirt pocket, he tapped the pack on the side of his hand until two filter-tipped ends popped forward. Turning the pack toward her, he offered, "Have one?"

She eyed heaven. "Do you know what I'm getting ready to do?"

He snorted out a short laugh. "Right." Pulling one out for himself, he stuck it in the corner of his mouth and dropped the pack into his pocket. "It's like this,

Cara.'' The cigarette bobbed up and down as he talked. ''I've got a chunk of money riding on you, and it'll increase my odds considerable if I let you in on the deal.''

''Oh, the bet.'' She crossed her arms before her. ''I guess everybody at the club is betting on one or the other of us. But if you're Martin's friend, I'm surprised that you're betting on me to win.''

He was in the process of lighting his cigarette. One hand held a lighted match while the other shielded the flame from the breeze. His brows were knit in concentration, but after she spoke, he squinted sideways at her.

''Umm.'' Shaking his head, he puffed on the cigarette. ''Not that bet, honey. No offense, but you ain't got no more chance of winnin' against Mart than a three-legged dog.''

She flinched at the lazy assurance in his drawl. ''How could I possibly take offense at that?'' she asked sarcastically.

''You shouldn't. It's just a fact, like tornadoes in the spring. Some things gotta get blown away. Today, you will.'' Dropping the match, he took another drag before pulling the cigarette from his mouth and holding it pinched between his thumb and first finger. Cara watched in agitated silence as he blew a smoke ring over her head. He returned her direct look with a combination of pity and humor in his eyes. ''Me and Martin have a private little bet on you that has nothing to do with your talent at runnin'. More like his talent in the bedroom.''

Cara felt the blood drain from her face. In a hushed whisper she demanded, "What are you talking about, Mr.... Mr. Dunlap?"

"Bobby, ma'am." He put his cigarette-filled fingers to the brim of his hat. "Anyway, I want you to know I have faith in you, but I figure it won't hurt to tell you just what we're bettin' on." One side of his mouth lifted in a wry grin. "See, I've sorta been livin' vicariously through Martin for some years now, and I know that he has a pretty fair average at gettin' women to go to bed with him."

Cara swallowed. Her mind chided her with the question—how many other foolish women had he seduced before her? And since? Pulling her lips together, she worked at blocking the vision from her mind and stared up at Bobby, seeing only his face, hearing only his voice. As far as her senses were concerned, there was no one else on the street. "Go on," she breathed. "What about Martin's... talent?"

"Well, see, I bet Martin five hundred bucks that he couldn't get you into bed. But this here bet you two got goin', I mean you going' home with him and all, well, it's just too good a setup for Martin to miss on. Get my point?" He took another drag and waited for her to nod. She didn't oblige him.

Knocking the ashes from the end of the cigarette, he went on. "Anyhow, I figured if I told you—warned you—and hell, I don't care about the five hundred. I mean, if you can stay outa his bed, I'd be tickled to give you the five I'd have to give him if he got ya in."

He dropped the cigarette and crushed it under his heel. She knew how it felt.

He was talking. "I just wanta see Dante miss with one woman one time. And Cara, ma'am, from what I've heard about you, I figure you to be my best chance. What-da-ya say? Do you think for five hundred bucks you could resist that smooth-talking stud?"

Cara lifted an unsteady hand to her forehead. A five-hundred-dollar bet? Martin had bet this man five hundred dollars that he would not only beat her in the race but get her into his bed! It was one thing to threaten her with "catering," but it was another thing entirely to be such a braggart to bet money with his loud-mouthed buddies that he could seduce her!

But why shouldn't he make the bet? He'd done it before, why shouldn't he think he could get her into his bed again? How much money had he made this way—betting on his ability to seduce a women? How many reputations had he ruined with his games? She felt used, dirty. Martin Dante might be impeccable in his business dealings, but where women were concerned, he was a crawling snake! She closed her eyes, gulping down a sob that rose in her throat. Unable to speak, she just nodded.

She felt a thud on her arms as he patted her enthusiastically. "Hell, Cara, that's great. Between you and me, we'll cut that guy down a peg. I'm gonna love this!"

She blinked damp lashes up to look at him. "How..." she rasped, "How do you know I won't lie?"

He lifted a hand to his hat brim, pushing it down more securely. "I figured just tellin' ya about the bet would make you mad enough to resist even Dante's charm. Am I wrong?"

Her lips lifted in a devastatingly sad smile. "No, Mr. Dunlap. You aren't wrong. But..." She straightened her shoulders. "I still might beat him."

He scratched his cheek, smiling down at her as though she'd just made a joke. "Sure, honey." With a conspiratorial wink, he added, "I'll drop by your class with the money next week."

The money! She'd been so appalled to discover the nature of their bet, she hadn't considered the fact that he'd offered her five hundred dollars. With a shake of her head, she gripped his arm. The shock was wearing off, and in its place a growing fury blossomed. "If... I happen not to win, I don't want your money, Mr. Dunlap. Resisting Martin Dante's charms will be *my pleasure.*" The last two words were growled through clenched teeth.

He reached for his pack of cigarettes again, screwing up his face in a surprised half smile that held a trace of new respect. "The hell you say." Thumping the pack on his wrist, he nodded thoughtfully, speaking more to himself than to her. "The hell..."

Cara didn't wait to hear more; pivoting on her heels, she hurried away from him. It was time to engage the enemy and, hopefully, stomp him into a machismo pulp under her feet.

Chapter Twelve

Cara was walking back when the gun went off for the wheelchair racers. Craning her neck to get a better view, she realized she was just ahead of the starting position. Completely forgetting her own problems, she raised two thumbs-up signs toward the nine people in wheelchairs who were taking part in the fifteen-kilometer race, her eyes filling with tears of admiration for their indomitable spirit. She squared her shoulders. If they could do this, so could she. Every hill that was tough for her was going to be pure torture for them. "Go get 'em, guys!" Her encouraging yell was lost in the uproar as hundreds of other spectators standing at the starting line clapped and cheered them on their way.

"Cara." A hand took hers, turning her around. "Here you are." Martin's face held a trace of worry, but it vanished quickly. "I thought I'd never find you. Let's get our places." Without further preliminaries, he pulled her along, weaving through the crush of spectators that were crowded in front of the Performing Arts Center where the runners had packed the street for several blocks. There were signs posted at varying locations that held running speeds per mile. The first read Four Minute Mile; the second, Five Minute Mile; and then farther back, one read Six Minute Mile and so on all the way to Ten Minute Mile or Longer.

He turned to look at her. "How fast do you figure you can run the mile?"

She twisted her hand to gain her release, but he was holding her as though he were afraid she'd disappear if he let her go. With a grimace, she retorted, "I know exactly how fast I run the mile. We have to do it once a year at our aerobics clinics. I run it in five and a half minutes."

His lips parted slightly and he looked down at her in surprise. "Five and a half?"

"Yes? Why?"

His expression opened in a wide grin. "Well, well. This may be a race after all. I figured you to run about seven or eight minutes per."

She shook her head, eyeing him doubtfully. Her news hadn't sent him into quailing panic, but there was a spark of something new in his eyes. Could it be respect? Lifting her proud chin, she asked, "What do you run?"

He moved a muscular shoulder. "About that, too." Cocking his head, he indicated the five-minute mile marker. "I guess we belong here, then." He'd emphasized the word "belong" as though he had planned to sacrifice his place closer to the front to be with her, a block or so farther back.

They squeezed out onto the street. Cara couldn't imagine how people so tightly packed could do anything but trip and fall, let alone run! "Okay," he began, seeming to read her mind. "When the gun goes off, just keep pace with the pack. In a block or so, they'll start spreading out." He let go of her hand and draped his arm casually about her shoulder, leaning down to whisper in her ear, "Some of the people who start up here are no more five-minute milers than Whistler's mother, so they'll be dropping back fairly quickly—especially after a couple of miles."

She swallowed, looking down at her watch. Three minutes until nine. Nodding, she acknowledged his counsel. Though the idea of sparring with him entered her mind, she decided that the wise move at this point was to save all her energy for the run.

She looked over at Martin. He was staring at his watch. As he stood there, his legs braced wide, Cara couldn't help but notice how powerfully he was built. His shoulders and arms were solid muscle, without a spare ounce of flesh. He was wearing a nylon-and-mesh tank top of light blue that hugged his chest like a jealous lover, leaving no need to imagine the broad masculine contours beneath the fabric. His race number was fastened to the front of the shirt just below the chest, just as hers and nearly twelve thousand others were. The see-through mesh of the lower half of his shirt fit snugly to his waist, where it was tucked into matching running shorts. She scanned the slender hips, covered in lightweight nylon. She knew how those hips felt, warm and firm, and she remembered how smoothly they moved, naked above her. Sucking in her cheeks, she bit down on the flesh, hoping the pain would blot out the unruly memory.

Martin shifted his weight, and without the strength to turn away, she continued to watch his lower extremities, as long muscles across his furred thighs bulged and flexed with the movement. He was wearing white jogging shoes and no socks. She moved her eyes to compare his new shoes to her own. She'd had them nearly a year. They were scuffed, dusty and— untied? "Oh dear," she breathed, dropping to repair the damage.

"It's time for the gun, Cara. Hurry," Martin called down to her, when she ducked out from under his arm. Just as he finished, there was a loud blast from a tenth-floor balcony of the Williams Plaza Hotel, where Tulsa's mayor shot off the starting gun.

"God!" she cried, pulling the laces and hoping she'd gotten them tight enough to last 9.3 miles. A fist grabbed her at the elbow and yanked her up just in time to keep her from being trampled to death.

She stumbled forward feeling sandwiched as she managed to regain her balance. Anxiety sparking in her eyes, she turned to look at Martin. She just might owe the man her life. The word "thanks" was wavering on the tip of her tongue when he shouted over the din, "Don't worry. We'll get out of this mess." He let go of her arm. "Once we do, find a comfortable pace and stick with it. We've got a long way to go."

Her desire to say thank-you died a quiet death as the reality of the race loomed before her. She shook her head. "The only pace I'm sticking with will be yours," she shouted back, turning away to look directly into the neck of the man six inches in front of her.

They'd started on Third Street. By the time they'd turned on Houston and made it to Fourth, the endless sea of green Tulsa Run T-shirts, multicolored outfits and name-brand running shoes was spreading out as Martin had predicted, with about seventy runners setting a quick pace. Cara didn't speak to Martin, and he didn't speak to her as they jogged along. But she kept his blue shorts in her peripheral vision. Martin made no pretense of ignoring her as she was him. He looked over at her often, probably judging her condition. By the time they reached the Eleventh-Street Bridge, spectators were yelling incentives for them to go faster. Easy for them to say, Cara groused inwardly. She was breathing fine, so far, in rhythm with her jogs. One inhale and one exhale for every eight steps. She was doing fine. Skimming a look at Martin from under her lashes she could tell that, unfortunately, he was, too. Cara glanced about her. Runners were joking and talking. Apparently, the easy part was not yet over.

By the time they reached the midway point at Forty-seventh Street and Riverside Drive, many of the runners were silent. Sweat beaded on faces and a few could be heard breathing heavily. Cara's hair was wet around her face, but she was still counting out her steps and breathing rhythmically. They made the turn back toward the finish. Cara forgot that she was ignoring Martin and looked over at him. He was watching her. When she met his gaze, he smiled and gave her a reassuring nod. "This is it, Beatrice," he mouthed.

Beatrice! She clamped her jaws shut. He was telling her she was going to lose! With a new burst of determination she put on steam. They'd been passing people all along, but with the added energy of his low challenge, she was running at a pace not easy to match—or sustain, for four and a half more miles.

Martin's frown told her that he knew that, too. Inwardly she smiled, as she pulled out in front of him. Maybe age would tell in this thing after all.

"Here!" Cara had been concentrating so hard on her breathing and her pace, she hadn't realized that Martin had come up beside her. He was tapping her shoulder. She looked over to see a paper cup about half full of sloshing water. "Have a drink," he offered in a husky command.

Licking her dry lips, she took it. "Thanks." Her voice was just as raspy. Slowing slightly, she downed the cool water. It was ambrosia. A few hundred feet down the road, she reached out and grabbed another cup from a volunteer manning one of the water stations along the route. That would help with the final push.

At the Twenty-first Street Bridge on the way back, Cara noticed that most of the sounds were of footsteps pounding away on asphalt, occasional comments from supportive spectators and the heavy breathing of runners straining to finish. She had to admit, if only to herself, that she was having trouble keeping her mind on her pace and her breathing. She could feel her heart thudding against her ribs. Things were not going quite so well. Sweat trickled down between her breasts and her back, cooling her.

She could see a wet trail down Martin's back, too. He was working damned hard to keep this pace....

"Martin's *back*! How did he get ahead of her? She closed her eyes for a split second of high anxiety. Damn him! She wasn't sure she could catch up now. Her legs hadn't been responding as well as they should for the past couple of miles.

"Cara, this is it. The Hill," Martin called over his shoulder, motioning ahead toward Fourteenth Street and Houston Avenue. He looked slightly worried. "Just do your best. You've done damn well. Don't kill yourself."

Kill herself? She would if she had to! She raised her hands over her head and inhaled deeply, completely filling her lungs several times. As Cara started up the Hill, she recalled what a cardiologist had told her once while she was taking a treadmill test. He'd said that every time the incline was increased by ten degrees, it was like putting a ten-pound bag of groceries in each arm. She inhaled deeply, not sure she had the strength to carry the weight of her own hands, let alone twenty pounds of groceries, but that couldn't be helped. Martin was ahead of her. And she couldn't let him finish that way!

Digging in, she plowed forward with all the might her exhausted body could muster. The crowd had increased measurably as they neared the finish, and they were cheering. They were shouting encouraging things like, "You can make it!" "You're almost there!" "Good going!" She even heard one lone female wail, *"Go get 'em, Rhythmic Aerobics!"*

That did it! A surge of pride fed her flagging muscles, and she was suddenly flying. Her lungs burned, and her legs ached. Her heels felt as if they were made of raw meat. With every crash into the hard pavement they screamed up at her to end the punishment and lie down.

But Martin was still ahead. Ever ahead. Just ahead! Every time she felt as though she were gaining, he sprinted a foot farther, widening the gap. "Damn... you... Martin... Dante!" she rasped. *"Damn!"* She could feel tears well up in her eyes, and she blinked them away. The platform that held the large flashing time board loomed one hundred yards ahead of them. Race assistants stood at each gate shouting out the official time of each runner who passed through.

At fifty feet from the finish, she was on Martin's heels. Thirty feet ahead of her out of the corner of her eye, she caught the movement of race attendants as they carried a stretcher onto the road where a man had fallen. As she ran, she watched as he rose to his knees. When Cara neared him, she could hear his wheezing refusal to be helped off the street. Waving the stretcher bearers back, he croaked, "I want to finish." A cheer went up from the crowd as he struggled, stumbling toward a gate. As Cara passed him, she called, "You got it, babe!" And then with one last leap she hurled herself across the finish line slamming into Martin's back.

The gate attendant yelled, "Time! Fifty-three minutes twenty-two! But Cara barely registered the fact. Louder in her ears was the "Woofff!" of sound as Martin absorbed the shock of her attack. She grabbed his neck to keep from falling to her face on the pavement. He grabbed her arms, too, where they crossed his shoulders. She wasn't sure if he was trying to help, or just attempting to keep from being strangled. After dragging her several feet farther, he slowed enough to pull her around to his side and transfer his hold to her waist. He kept moving at a fairly rapid clip, half dragging her along. They were in one of the eight narrow lanes that had been cordoned off by rope, for the purpose of funneling runners away from the finish line where thousands of runners would continue to come barreling through, each in a final spurt of speed, for another hour or so.

He took her firmly by the arm and walked her to the end of the block where the roped aisles ended, and he kept walking with her until they had crossed the street and were again standing on the edge of the Williams

Center Green. Taking both of her arms, he turned her to him. His face was streaming with sweat, and his hair was windswept and glistening wet. Whether she liked it or not, he was beautiful. With an edge of concern in his voice he asked, "You okay?"

She sagged against him; her body had no strength left to do as she bid it. Angry that she was beaten—and beat—she balled her hands and reached up to listlessly pummel his chest. "I...I...*hate*...you!" she croaked between labored breaths, wishing it were true. "I hate...*you*!"

He circled her waist, guessing that if he did not, she would sag to the street. "I know, I know," he soothed. "But, you were wonderful, Cara. I only beat you by three seconds."

Her eyes flew to his face. It was a blur. "Three? Three...lousy..." She hit his chest again and sagged farther, her knees buckling.

"You're going to fall."

"Let me! I...want to!" She spread her hands on his chest, looking up pleadingly. "Just let me sink to my...knees...my forehead on the sidewalk. Throw—" She sucked in a ragged breath, moaning. "Throw cement on me. I'll be a memorial to the Agony of...Defeat." She shook her head in distress, squeezing her eyes shut. "They can put... bronze...plaque on the soles of my feet." The last words came out in a whimper. "Call me The Unknown Jogger."

His arms tightened, and so did his voice. "Cut it out, Cara. Straighten up. You didn't lose anything!

Not really. I bet you came in one of the top ten women runners in the whole damn race. When they publish your time in tomorrow's paper, no one will ever dare call aerobics class 'jiggling' again.'' He moved his hands to her arms, gripping tightly. "So quit whining. You should be damned proud of yourself. I'm proud of you.''

His harsh tone startled her out of her funk, and she felt new strength in her knees. Eyeing him narrowly, she tried to absorb what he had just said. Did he really mean that about her time? She had no idea what was good and what was only fair. Did she really do that well?

She had just stood there, staring up at him for a full minute. His lips twitched and lifted in a crooked grin, a chuckle rumbling deep in his chest. "The Unknown Jogger?'' He shook his head, his silvery eyes never leaving hers. "The things you can come up with.'' Touching her back, he took charge. "Let's go home in your car. I came in a cab.''

She stiffened at his touch, and the reminder of what was yet before her. "Cab? Why?'' she questioned, her voice weak and thready.

His touch became firmer, settling just above the outward curve of her hips. "I figured if I let you drive back alone, you'd try to escape across the border.''

"What border?'' she challenged, trying to make it sound as though the thought had never occurred to her.

Watching her beneath skeptically lowered lids he bent his head toward her ear and answered huskily, "Any border."

A quaint kitchen clock chimed five times, and Cara eyed it with a caustic hatred that might have stopped a less stout-hearted timepiece. "Oh, shut up. I know what time it is. Martin just dragged me over here, remember?"

She had to admit, though grudgingly, that he'd been lenient, letting her go home, bathe, change and take a long nap. Surprisingly, even in her troubled state, she'd slept soundly. Her head had dropped to the pillow at noon, and the next thing she was conscious of was Martin's knock at her door at four forty-five.

Quickly, she'd jumped into a short-sleeved sweatsuit. As she'd laced up a pair of tennis shoes, she'd mumbled to herself that she was damned if she was going to dress up for her servitude. And she certainly didn't intend to look in any way fetching!

She had to admit, though, Martin's kitchen was a most attractive slaughterhouse to be led to. She wiped her hands on a terry towel and walked to the refrigerator. Opening it, she shook her head. It held everything from light cream to something that, if she'd had to take a stab at it, she'd have guessed to be truffles. But she hoped her life would never depend on it. Picking up a jar, she read, Marinated Artichoke Hearts. With a wry twist of her lips, she mused darkly that this was certainly a culinary necessity—if you happened to be making Marinated Artichoke Heart Burgers.

Putting it back on the shelf, she shook her head. So far she'd found nothing that she recognized as eatable food—nothing was instant; no frozen entrées, no canned chili or stew, not even any semi-instant meals, like boxed pasta, with instructions that lightheartedly stated, "just add ground beef."

"Martin," she complained loud enough to be heard in the living area. "How do you expect me to cook you a dinner in a kitchen so ill-equipped?"

He appeared at the door, looking exceedingly fresh and well groomed in a pair of beige cotton slacks and a cream-colored knit shirt. Leaning a shoulder against the doorjamb, he grinned at her pouting expression. "Cara, Phillip came over here last night and brought enough food to keep us well-fed through an Antarctic winter. What do you need?"

She leaned back against the counter. "For starters, a couple years' apprenticeship with Julia Child!" She tossed an emphatic finger to the floor. "Get Phillip over here. I need someone to transform these—raw materials into usable products. He can make something and freeze it, and I'll thaw it out."

"Phillip is on his way to Paris."

She planted her hands on her hips. "That's no excuse. Get him back here now, or the deal's off."

He struggled with the urge to laugh. Clearing his throat, he suggested mildly, "You're grasping at straws, love. Don't worry about me. I'll like anything you come up with."

Before she had a chance to suggest that he might later have a need to reexamine his options—after her rat poison soup du jour—he was gone. Mumbling under her breath, she vowed that he was not going to get away with this treatment of her! If he'd lost, he would have had no intention of coming to her class in a clown suit! And, by the same token, she had no intention of... of cooking... or anything else for him! Her conversation with Bobby Dunlap reared its ugly head in her memory. Curling her fingers in a death grip around the counter's edge, she vowed that Martin Dante would pay for that little bit of side wagering, or her name wasn't Professor Cara Torrence!

The question was, *how* could she annihilate him? She kept seeing a vivid and satisfactory picture of Martin with a full meal dumped over his head, but the aftermath of ruined rugs and furniture that belonged to a perfectly nice couple like the Huerters put a definite damper on the savoring of her revenge. So, how was she going to give him what he deserved and still protect the belongings of innocent people?

In her mental wanderings she found herself in front of the pantry staring at its door. Uninterested, she opened it. Foreign items that probably had something to do with cooking stared back at her—baking soda and powder, several colors of oils and syrups, brown rice, bags of beans, cans of clams, caviar and water chestnuts. There was even a jar of pickled peaches and a box of white raisins. What did a person make with all that? What would even possess anyone to go to so much trouble just to eat? Standing back, she crossed her arms, screwing up her mouth in disgruntled thought. Maybe she could whip up a dinner of raw beans and caviar served over white raisins, and for dessert, something light—like a clam and marinated artichoke cake? She shook her head. Not deadly enough.

Her eyes fell on a wooden bin in the bottom of the pantry. It looked like it held potatoes. Potatoes? She knew how to boil potatoes. She even knew that from boiled potatoes, mashed potatoes came! A smile blossomed from her scowl. Mashed potatoes would make a most satisfactory revenge. She pictured Martin covered in gooey, sticky potatoes! What an ingenious idea for dinner—Martin Dante and gravy! With a satisfied nod, she couldn't help but wonder what Martin might say if he knew that he was about to become the main course?

She plucked an armload of the starchy weapons from the bin. It didn't matter at this moment that her plan was not completely worked out. By the time she had a gallon or so mashed, she'd have come up with a devious strategy worthy of her anger.

"Something smells good." Martin appeared at the door. "Dinner about ready?"

She smothered a grin and straightened her face before turning around. "Uh-huh. I have some potatoes cooking—be another twenty minutes or so." She didn't say that she'd already made four batches. She'd mixed as many as the mixer could hold at a time, and hidden them under the sink in a large broiler pan.

"Good." He nodded, smiling. It was such an un-suspecting and innocent smile, she almost, but not quite, felt a twinge of guilt. "I thought you might like to come in and see the debate, if you've got some time."

"The debate?" Donnelly and Andrew Mathison! She'd almost forgotten. "Oh, yes. I wouldn't dare miss it." Wiping her hands on a towel, she scurried by him. "The timer will go off when they're done."

He followed, taking a seat on the couch next to her. She sat back and shifted a sardonic look toward him. "Are you sure you ought to watch this? We might sway you our way."

"I'll chance it." He sat back, resting an arm along the back of the couch. When he smiled at her, she turned abruptly away to watch as the men were intro-duced. Though she pretended to be totally absorbed in the introductions, she couldn't ignore the radiant heat of his skin as it warmed her shoulders. She sat forward, resting her elbows on her knees. Deciding to put verbal distance between them as well, she gouged, "Honestly, Martin. I can't understand how you could know anything about the candidates and not have an opinion. Surely, working with both Donnelly and Mathison, you've seen which man is better...oh—" she held up a finger as though he had been the one speaking "—they're coming on. Quiet."

"Yes, dear."

She tilted him a brief, dark look before losing her-self in the clash of candidates. When it was over, she relaxed back against his arm. "Here, here, Donnelly.

I guess you told him!" Turning to a silent Martin, she challenged, "Well? Don't you think Donnelly came through that way out in front? Admit it. He's definitely the better man."

Martin's expression held high amusement, and his mercury eyes glistened with fun. "I think Donnelly could have fallen off the podium in a drunken stupor and you would still have been impressed. You're far from objective on the subject." She opened her mouth, but he held up a halting hand. "Why don't we just wait and see what the rest of the state thinks?"

A buzzer went off in the kitchen, and Cara remembered her crusade to bury Martin in his own mashed potatoes. She jumped up, losing any desire to fight, the sweet smell of victory filling her nostrils. "Potatoes!" she stated, as though it were a call to battle.

Martin stood, too. "Good. I've got some repair work to finish up in the bathroom. Let me know when the food is on the table."

A light went on in her brain. The bathroom! That would be the perfect place to douse him. Very hurriedly, she whipped the last batch into a frothy paste. By the time she had it lopped onto the rest of the white mountain, she could hardly carry it. But, no matter, strength came with determination. And her adrenaline flowed freely now that retribution was in sight!

Chapter Thirteen

Martin. Dinner's ready. Why don't you wash up?''

There was a brief pause as she heard something being put down with a light thunk. "Great. I'll be right there,'' he called as she stood, plastered against the hall wall, waiting to make sure that he was in the bathroom. After a couple of seconds, she peeked in the door. Craning her neck, she could see the reflection of his hands as he lathered them under the tap. Now was her chance!

Tiptoeing on her silent tennis soles, she stealthily edged her way along the wall toward the bathroom, her heart pounding and her arms aching from the weight of her burden. She had to make her attack swift and on target. As she reached the door, she decided that she'd increase her odds for success if she shut it behind her. So, with one last deep breath, she pivoted into the open doorway, curling her toes around the edge of the door and swinging it closed as she dashed in.

She only saw Martin's face for a split second as his head swung around in surprise. Then the pan of potatoes was up and over his head. "What the—" His aborted question held a sharp edge of surprise as he flung an elbow up to deflect the white blob that was coming at him.

Cara didn't expect his quick defense, and when he hit the pan with his arm part of the contents were knocked back in her direction, splashing her face and chest with clods of warm potatoes. The wet food made damp glopping sounds as it hit her hair and face. She had to close her eyes to keep from getting mashed potatoes in them. "Oh, no!" she cried, as the pan fell on her feet, still full enough to make her hop around the room in pain. "Ouch! Martin! That hurt!" she whimpered.

As it is sometimes with the fortunes of war, on the third hop, Cara landed in a puddle of potatoes, and her foot slid out from under her. She screamed as her feet skidded sideways into the bathtub, forcing her to fall back on her hip and one elbow.

She lay on her side, moaning, forgetting her revenge, wondering how it could have gone so wrong.

There was silence for a minute. And then Cara nearly jumped out of her skin at the sound of a guttural growl. She closed her eyes, grimacing at what

Martin, the enraged beast, would do to her, but before she had time to try to get up, the growl had become a deep, clear laugh that rang and echoed through the small room. "Oh, Cara!" He dropped to his knees, sliding an arm around her back, and helping her to a sitting position. "I should have known something like this would happen. You were giving up too easily. Are you all right?"

She opened her eyes in stunned surprise at the rich, amused timbre of his voice, but she didn't look at him. With a groan, she rubbed her lip. "No, I'm not. My back is broken."

She could hear him sit down beside her. His chuckle rumbled again. "Your back is no more broken than your spirit."

She felt his hand on her chin, turning her to face him. "Look what you've done to me, you little hell-cat."

Finally forced to view her handiwork, Cara's lips parted in a small "oh" of surprise. He looked like a melting snowman from his shoulders up. If it weren't for his long eyelashes, he wouldn't be able to see. His hair was covered with potatoes, and his shoulders held a pile of stuff two inches thick. But through it all, he was smiling at her, his eyes twinkling beneath the protective bridge of his lashes. "You little fool," he teased gently. With two fingers, he scooped some potato off her cheek and then moved his fingers up to her forehead, where he smoothed matted curls away from her eyes. "You crazy fool."

Sitting back on his haunches, he started to clear some of the mess from his own face. Licking his lips, he made a face. "This stuff is terrible."

She straightened, pointing a defiant, if potato spattered, chin at him. "I wasn't working for taste, Martin—merely texture."

He looked down at his hand, full of the mess, and rubbed his fingers together as if studying the consistency. "Hmm? Texture seems good—at least as good as any I've ever worn before."

She had to give him credit, he was certainly taking this better than she'd expected him to. With a small frown creasing her brow, she sat back on her heels, much the way he was. Looking down at herself, she shrugged, plucking at the wet cotton knit of her blouse. "Ugh." Putting her hand on the side of the tub for support she stood, wincing at the pain in her bruised hip. "Well, you have to admit that I did 'cook' dinner for you. You tasted it. So, I think I'll be going—to change out of the leftovers."

Martin's brow dipped. "What about this mess?" He spread his arms to indicate the tile floor that was covered with potatoes.

She shrugged, trying to appear as though the problem was solely his. "It doesn't matter what you do with it. Lock the door and leave it, for all I care."

He ran a hand across his mouth. Cara's frown deepened to see a new laughter glisten in his eyes as he rose to one knee then stood to tower over her. "You locked the door. Our only problem now is the leaving part." He indicated the door with a casual gesture.

Cara followed the movement, and her gaze came to a shocked halt where the doorknob was suppose to be. It wasn't there! She gasped. "What happened to the knob?" Panic rose in her throat, and without waiting for his response she slid to the door and pushed. It didn't budge. "What's wrong, Martin?" She flipped him a desperate look, her sticky hair slapping her shoulders as she did.

He shrugged, and a stream of potato slid down his broad chest. "That—my little potato head—is what I was repairing when you so inventively 'spilled' in here with today's special. The lock doesn't work. It needs a new part. I was just discovering that fact when you called me to dinner."

"Well?" She stepped away from the door and turned to face him, dropping a palm to the counter to keep from slipping on the slimy tiles. "Just put the knob back on and forget it for now."

He cocked his white head toward the bedroom beyond the door. "It's out there on the dresser. You go get it."

She bit her lip at the realization, gasping. "Then, you're saying we're locked in here?"

He crossed his arms, and leaned a hip on the counter. "Bright girl." He chuckled. "But there's really no problem. We've got food and water." With a swipe of his finger on his forehead, he dumped a dollop of potatoes in the sink before continuing. "We won't starve."

She made a disgusted face. "Martin. Don't joke. This isn't funny."

"It isn't?" He eyed her narrowly. "Where's your sense of humor?" Turning on the tap, he bent over the sink and dashed water on his face and hair until most of the mess was off. "How will we ever be able to tell this story and keep a straight face?" He took a towel from the rack and dried his face and hair as he went on. "How will anybody be able to hear it and not laugh? Face it, Cara. It's funny."

"Tell it!" she breathed. "Oh, no. Never in your life, Martin. Promise me you'll never tell anyone about this." She tried to walk to him to plead her case, but with her slippery shoes, she skidded on the first step and ran into his chest.

He circled her waist with his arms, and they came together like two gooey layers of the same dessert. Her head tilted back and she looked up, wide-eyed at his handsome face.

"There's no need to get rough," he murmured with a crooked grin, and then, without warning, he lowered his lips to hers.

Before she realized it, he was kissing her deeply, his tongue playing enticingly against the sensitive skin just inside her lips. His arms tightened, drawing her into his hard chest. Cara could feel the solid heat of his chest as he pressed her into him.

A moan escaped her throat as her body became charged with his touch, his kiss. Her mind fought what was happening, just as she had fought him for months. But she'd been successful only when she'd managed to remain at arm's length. Now, he was inside her barrier. His tongue, his hands and the desire she could feel in his extreme nearness all were wearing her down. The enemy had broken down the door, and she was without a weapon.

"Martin...Martin..." she breathed, her arms slipping up to circle his neck. "I...I missed you more than I planned to." She opened her eyes, and a lone tear slid down her cheek. "Why? Why do you do this to me?" she sobbed into his neck. "Why—"

"Shh." He kissed her cheek. Slipping a hand beneath her blouse, he explored her naked back, massaging and soothing the tensed muscles as he went. "Don't cry, Cara. It's not a sin to care about someone." He kissed her cheek, and then the top of her nose, murmuring small, gentling endearments as his lips sought hers again. This time when they met, hers were willing, and she was a sighing wanton in his arms. Their kisses became living things that took flight and soared, and their hands and arms became explorers in awe of the sensuous differences of each warm wilderness.

She felt Martin tremble and heard his groan. "Come with me," he ordered huskily as he lifted her up and over the tub rim, standing her inside the over-size square porcelain fixture. "Take off your clothes, Cara." He kissed her lightly on the lips as he stepped in beside her.

Feeling weak in the knees, she gaped at him, her body sizzling from and for his touch. She felt as though she'd been struck by lightning and left to die. "What?" she asked, her voice thready and high-pitched.

He was pulling his shirt off over his head. When he dropped it to the floor, he turned and gently lifted off her blouse before lowering his face to her upturned breasts. Kissing each rosy tip, he murmured, "Take off your clothes, love. You're a mess." The softness of his words, and the titillation of his lips and his tongue against her breasts set her womanly core to throbbing for him. But before she could do as he bid, his hands were already sliding the warm-up pants and her panties down her slender legs.

Lips trembling with anticipation, she put her hands on his shoulders to keep from falling with her own crazy weakness. As though in a trance, she lowered herself to sit on the tub's edge while he untied her shoes and tossed them one by one onto the floor. She was unaware of how long it took him to remove her clothes. She only knew that his hands were running lovingly along her bare hips and thighs. On his knees now, he circled her waist with his arms, drawing his face to her glowing skin. Nuzzling the softness of her stomach, he whispered, "What is it about you that makes me feel so alive?" He seemed to be truly disturbed by the question, and Cara looked down at him. She couldn't see his face. He was nipping at the tender skin below her navel, moving down.

As his kiss moved lower, she gasped, and a shudder of passion swept through her with the intimacy of his touch. "Cara, Cara..." he muttered, his arms trembling. "I have never known a woman like you."

She grasped his head to her, licking her lips, and sighing as he took her beyond time and space. Her breathing became rapid and shallow, and she whimpered his name as his kiss sent her spiraling beyond the earthbound summit, "Oh, God!" She cried out her release.

"Cara, you go through me like a tornado," Martin muttered in a passion-deepened whisper as he trailed kisses up her body to capture her lips again.

"Oh, Martin..." She hugged his broad, naked back, listening to his heart thud as wildly as her own.

There was a tiny, piercing scream in the back of her brain that warned her about not letting Martin take her and make love to her. But much louder and much stronger than that pitiful little warning cry was her deafening, thunderous need to take him inside and make him a vital part of her. He'd make her body sing with orgasmic release, and all that made her a woman cried out for more.

Though tears trembled at the corners of her eyes, her fingers stumbled over each other in their eagerness to get his clothes off. He saw her difficulty and helped, until at last, they were standing body to body in the tub. She thrilled at the feeling of his readied manhood as it pulsated against her inner thighs, caressing her with a touch that was light and yet so undeniable.

"Now, love—" He pressed himself against her, drawing a tremulous sigh. Kissing her shoulder, he leaned past her and turned on the shower. "Dessert."

Sliding his hands on her buttocks, he pressed her back into the tiled wall, giving them both support as he lifted her legs so that she could hold his waist in their possessive vise. As he did, Cara settled herself over his erect manhood.

He moved his hand around to hold her hips, slipping himself into her as she curled her legs tightly about him. Both of them moaned in concert at the delight of their joining, and Cara held him with all her strength, glorying at the depth of his possession.

She kissed his wet chest, circling her tongue within the glistening mat of hair. He smelled sweet and clean. He felt slick, warm and hard. She clung to his neck and pressed more deeply into him with every exhilarating thrust of his hips, sighing with the feeling it precipitated.

His large hands held her securely to him, directing each rhythmic plunge so that it would be more thrilling than the last, until she cried out, her fingers grasping the silky hair at his nape. Her head lolled against the tiles and water pelted her burning face as pulsating waves of feeling burst her body apart in a wonderful and terrible rending.

Martin's shudder, and his hands holding the soft flesh of her hips told her that he had found his release, too. With a low moan, he bent his head, laying his lips against the hollow of her throat. He groaned her name, pulling her to him with quivering arms. "Cara, Cara..." he sighed against her skin. "Don't run away from me tonight."

She lowered her legs from his back, and he held her to him until her toes touched the tub floor. She regretted the separation of their bodies so much that she held tight to his neck. With a gentle, sated sigh, she nuzzled her cheek in the mat of soft hair at his chest. "Isn't that a moot point, darling? We're locked in here, remember?"

There was a rumble in his chest that went all the way through her. He was laughing. She looked up at his face, smiling at his handsome grin. "See. You had forgotten."

He shook his head. "Where there's a will, my love, there's a way." Taking her wrists, he gently pulled her hands away from him. He stooped down and scooped up the abandoned bar of soap. "Here. I'll be right back." He pushed the glass door open and walked to the counter beside the sink. Cara peeped out, curious to see what he was doing. She was surprised to see him pick up a screwdriver. She hadn't seen that before. Stepping carefully between globs of potatoes, he made it to the door without mishap. Bending so that the hole where the knob should have been was at his eye level, he stuck the tip of the screwdriver into the workings. There was a click, and the door swung open easily.

Cara's gasp made Martin slant a worried look over his shoulder. He stood and turned quickly as Cara stepped out of the running shower. "Why, you..." She tipped hurt eyes up to his solemn face. "Why did you say we were locked in if it was that easy to get out?"

"I could lie and say I wasn't sure the screwdriver would work." He shrugged a muscled shoulder. "The truth is, I knew you'd run away if I opened the door."

She balled her fists. "*Get* away, you mean! Why did you have to lie, Martin? Why must you always—"

"Cara, I just wanted to—" He was holding up a placating hand.

"I *know* what you wanted!" Stiffly, she began to edge toward the door. Her insides were tied in knots, and her pulse raced. His broad frame was blocking the door. How was she going to escape? In her frustration and desperation, she blurted something she hadn't intended to say, "Damn you and your manipulating! Bobby Dunlap told me about your little side bet! He told me that you'd get five hundred of his dollars if you got me into your bed. But don't worry, I think you can still get your money. The actual location is a minor technicality, I'm sure." Her voice broke, but she squared her shoulders, trying to carry off her brave pose. "He thought I might be the one woman who could resist you . . . your . . ." She bit her lip to stop its quivering. "I . . . I guess he . . . we both underestimated you." With one furious push against his stone-hard chest, she struggled past him toward the bedroom door. Just as she reached it, she realized that she couldn't leave his condominium naked and dripping wet.

Swiveling toward his closet, she threw open the door, grabbed one of his shirts and was throwing it across her shoulders when he reached her, taking both of her wrists. The shirt fell to the floor. "What are you babbling about, Cara? What five hundred dollars?" His eyes were penetrating, sharp and probing. He was a fine actor, too, it appeared. He actually looked as if he didn't know what she was talking about.

Enraged that he couldn't even admit his guilt when faced with it, she growled like a wounded lioness, pulling her hands from his grasp. "Don't insult me by denying it, Martin. Just let me go." Tears sparkled on her lower lashes as she slashed out a wild, frustrated hand, striking him across the right cheek—the cheek that when he smiled held the damned beautiful, slashing dimple. She cursed him foully under her breath as she grabbed up the shirt and wrapped it about her. Thank God it was dark outside. No one would see her escape up the steps to her own place, disheveled and half dressed.

As she spun from a stunned Martin, she choked out a devastated cry. "You won, Martin! You won the race. You won...everything! I hope it makes you happy!"

She was hurting. She'd been hurting since the scene in Martin's bedroom. Hoping that she was wiping away the tear unnoticed, she jammed her thumb down on the stopwatch and shouted a little louder than necessary, "Pulse! Go!" The class walked about the room as they counted out their pulse beats. Her eyes were glued on the digital face as it clicked out every second. It was almost too blurry to see. "Stop! Okay, cool-down dance." Mechanically, she flicked the music on, her memory slipping back to yesterday and her twenty-four hours of solitary misery.

She'd stayed in her room, slugging her pillow and trying to find one good reason not to cry. It really hurt, considering all that Martin had done to prove how little she really meant to him—but, damn the man, she was still in love with him! With everything else he'd done to her, he'd also taken her heart and stuffed it, uncaring, in his hip pocket.

And what was worse, in her desolation, she'd had at least ten calls from her students who'd seen her race standings in the paper, asking about the cooking and catering payment. She'd been vague, saying she'd cooked him a dinner, and the debt was paid.

Lucy had called her, her newly born twins crying to be fed in the background. She'd announced in a huff that she was surprised that Martin had insisted that she go through with the payment. He was the only man at the health club who had. Apparently, all the men who'd bet against her had opted not to make the women pay off. According to Lucy, they'd said, "If Cara Torrence, who's never run a race, could place seventh among all the women running, then they could forget the bet."

So Martin had been right about that, too. He'd said she'd come in among the top ten women. His predictions about everything, as well as his assurance about his own sexual power, seemed to be one hundred percent on target. She just wondered if he'd predicted that she would fall in love with him, too? Probably. No doubt he knew the effect he had on women by now.

Cara was relieved that class was about over, and she could escape to be alone. She needed time to mend. She hoped no one guessed how tattered she was inside, and what colossal effort it had taken for her to come here today.

As usual, there were a number of men watching the class, but this time, there was something subtly different in the way they were watching. There were no snide snickers or guttural asides. They were quietly attentive, almost respectful. A melancholy smile lifted her lips. That, at least, was the one positive result of this whole miserable fiasco.

A tittering and giggling pulled Cara from her ragged attempts to concentrate on the memorized steps, and she lifted a curious gaze toward the mirrored wall to look at her class. Some of them nearer the front where she was were still dancing, but those nearer the back were watching something behind the weight equipment. The men were staring outright.

Cara stopped dancing and turned to see what they were laughing at. Ducking to look around a wall of poles and weights, she saw a glimpse of red, and she heard an odd jingling that was getting louder.

The women were backing away and casting furtive glances toward her. Cara's throat went dry with apprehension, and she caught a student's eye. "What is it, Lucy?" she asked in a cautious whisper.

Lucy, who'd come for a visit, was leaning against a wall, a half-eaten candy bar in her hand. Rolling her eyes, she laughed. "Cara, not in a million years would I have believed this."

Cara spread her hands in exasperation. "Believed wh—" Her throat closed, her hands dropped to her sides and her knees turned to soft butter. "Martin?" Her voice quivered with utter amazement. There before her was the tallest, most endearing clown she had ever seen.

He was dressed in a red suit covered with big yellow polka dots. A stiff white collar flopped with every step he took toward her, and his hands were lost in huge yellow gloves. His feet were also yellow, and as big as boats. A red clown hat, covered with tiny bells, sat jauntily on the side of his head, the tassel grazing his shoulder. His face was not painted, but beneath low slung lids, there was a glistening sadness in his eyes. And below those eyes, where his straight nose should have been, was a red ball.

"Martin…" she whispered as he reached her, "what are you doing?"

"Cara, I—" He started to touch her arm, but looked down at his imprisoned hands. Tugging at the gloves, he pulled them off and dropped them at her feet. Cara had been watching his face, and when she saw him wince, she dropped her gaze to his hands. The right one was wrapped in a gauze bandage. With a gasp, she tentatively took it into both of hers. "What happened to you?"

For the first time, he smiled. It was a weary expression. "Yesterday, Bobby Dunlap…explained what he'd done." From a huge pocket, he pulled out a folded piece of paper. "This is for you."

With her hand poised over the paper, her eyes shot first to the gauze-wrapped fist and then back up to his face. "You…you hit him? For telling me about the bet?" She ran a distracted hand through her hair. "Oh Martin, you shouldn't have—"

"Just read it." He dropped his eyes to the paper. "Bobby wasn't a happy man when he wrote it—but while his jaw is wired he won't be able to talk very well."

She gasped. "Don't tell me you broke his jaw! You?"

The laugh that rose in his throat held no humor, and he flexed his wounded hand. "I didn't mean to. But now that it's done, I think a wired jaw might do Bobby some good."

She took the note, unfolding it. "What is this—a subpoena?"

"An apology—actually a confession."

She scanned the words Bobby had scrawled.

Then a surprising fact hit her. In the note, Bobby admitted goading Martin with a bet the morning of the fifth of July. The fifth? That had been only days before she had actually gone to bed with Martin the first time. Apparently, at the Run Bobby hadn't known that. Martin had never told Bobby!

Her hand began to shake with relief. At least, Martin hadn't agreed to the bet. Her eyes scanned the written words again. "So, back on the fifth of July you told him to take his five hundred dollars and go to hell?" Lifting a grateful smile to his face, she whispered, "Thank you for that, anyway." She crumbled the note in her hand, holding onto it for dear life. "But why the clown suit, Martin? You didn't lose."

"I hope you're right." He took her into his arms, and as he did, she could hear a murmur go up among the men and women watching from the perimeter of the room. Martin didn't seem to notice, as he pulled her against him and whispered huskily, "But since you left me Saturday night, I've felt like the world's biggest loser."

She closed her eyes and inhaled the clean, musky smell that belonged only to him. Even through the baggy suit, she could feel the masculine hardness of his chest, and the heavy beat of his heart. "Cara," he rasped near her ear, "I don't want to look around one day and find myself back in a world without clowns."

She felt the silent, almost pleading inspection of his gaze, and lifted glistening eyes to meet his. Mercury fire smoldered over her face, making her catch her breath with its intensity. Reaching up, she plucked the red ball from his straight, beautiful nose. "What do you mean, Martin?" she breathed, almost too quietly to be heard.

"I mean there's only one thing worse than being a fool, and that's being nobody's fool. I've been nobody's fool for too long. I love you, Cara. I want to be yours.

"I want grass skirts and cases of fluorescent spray paint in my bedroom closet. I want you to decorate the master bath with any damn kind of food you get the urge to throw. I..." His voice cracked, and she was astonished to see a glisten of high emotion in his eyes. "Cara, I don't care if you cook. I don't want you to change. I just want you to do what you do best." He kissed her temple, and as he spoke, his lips delighted the sensitive skin. "I want you to be you. All I ask is that you do it—with me."

Cupping her face in his hands, he tilted it so that his inviting lips hovered a hairbreadth away from hers. Cara forgot where she was, and didn't care. As she lifted a welcoming kiss to his mouth, one of the less subtle men in the room began to cough loudly. With a start she drew away, her face coloring with embarrassment. But before she could retreat more than a step, Martin pulled her back. "No, you don't. I'm not leaving this room until you tell me how you feel about what I've said. Look—" His voice shook slightly as he made a very visible effort to control himself. "I figure you've pretended to be tough because you're afraid. I know under all those spikes you throw you're soft and warm and terribly vulnerable, and you're afraid to let any man get close because you've been hurt." His searching look was earnest, tender.

"Marry me, Cara, and you'll never have to be afraid again. I'll never hurt you, never try to make you something you aren't. I just want to love you."

His lips grazing hers were so compelling that she had no strength or desire to draw away—not now, not ever again. "Oh, Martin," she whimpered, unable to take her eyes off his sleepy, sensuous eyes. "Yes...oh, yes, I will...."

His soft smile was like the dawn of a perfect day. As he took her into his embrace and kissed her warmly, shouts and cheers went up around them, and wolf whistles filled the large hall. "All right!" "Way to go!" "Another one bites the dust!" were some of the shouted observations tossed out by their audience.

Cara moaned with embarrassment against his lips. Her face flushed at the commotion that his unconventional proposal was causing. With a reassuring squeeze, Martin pulled away from her, but didn't quite relinquish his hold. "Let's get out of here," he murmured, brushing her lips tenderly with his own.

She was so breathless, she could only nod. Pulling her securely to him, his arms around her shoulders, he led her away, oblivious to the whooping melee they were leaving behind.

Once inside Martin's car, she tugged the hat from his head, caressing it against her cheek. "Martin?" She slid him a fluttery, uncharacteristically shy look. "Now that we're going to be..."

His hand went to the back of her neck, and he lovingly tangled his fingers in her hair. "Married, Cara. You can say the word if you really try." Leaning over the central console, he lightly tasted her lips. "Say it."

She dropped the hat in her lap and drew him as close as she could over the stick shift. With her tongue teasing his opened lips, she murmured, "Married..." She smiled against his firm, warm mouth, feeling a great weight drop from her shoulders. Martin wanted her just as she was! No changes! He wanted a clown. A noncook. He wanted Professor Cara Torrence!

With a laugh gurgling in her throat, she drew back and sighed. Still smiling, she allowed her eyes to wander over him adoringly. She loved every chiseled line of his face, his thick, straight hair with its distinguished silver streak, the formidable breadth of his shoulders. Feeling finally free to speak the truth, she admitted a little breathlessly, "Martin—I think I've loved you almost all my life. I've tried not to, but . . ."

He sat back, looking strikingly handsome in his surprise. "What?"

She took his hand in her lap, stroking it lovingly. "Do you remember using the phone in a little grocery store one night after the Cinderella Ball—somebody had taken the tires off your car?"

His eyes narrowed as she went on. "A girl was in that store, with mud on her face? You said she was a sight. . . ."

He leaned closer, his expression opening in recognition. "You were that girl."

She nodded, her cheeks growing hot.

He put a finger under her chin, turning her face from one side to the other, pretending to examine her with a critical eye. "I should have remembered. Even streaked with dirt, that was one of the most striking faces I'd ever seen. It hasn't changed that much."

She drew away from his touch, recalling the incident fully, now. Even after all this time, it still stung her pride. Lowering her lashes, she reminded, "You called me 'a sight.' That hurt for a long time."

There was a moment of silence before he took her face between his large, warm hands. "My God, Cara. I had no idea you took it that way. I meant to compliment you—you were a lovely young girl." He shook his head, covering her hand with his. "My only defense is, I was mad as hell at Bobby Dunlap at the time—"

"Bobby Dunlap?" she asked incredulously. "Did he do it? The same practical joker who—"

"Has promised to move to the opposite side of the street when he sees me coming," Martin finished for her, an edge of irritation in his voice. "I don't know why I put up with him all these years without breaking his jaw before." With a wry smile and a meaningful glance, he added, "Maybe it was because he never hurt someone I loved before."

His soft words made Cara too happy to be angry, even at Bobby Dunlap. Cuddling as close as she could to him, she surprised herself by pleading Bobby's defense. "Don't be too hard on him, Martin. After all, he did bring us together." She leaned against his chest, looking appealingly up into his silvery eyes. She smiled slowly, sensuously, feeling a new, trusting confidence grow inside her. "Maybe we ought to make him our best man," she teased.

Martin grunted. "He'd probably handcuff himself to you and we'd all have to spend our honeymoon together."

She giggled, feeling wonderful in the encompassing warmth of his arms. Tracing his chin with her finger, she agreed, "You're probably right. But wouldn't it be a great story to tell our kids?"

His chuckle rumbled against her cheek before he remarked dryly, "No."

She fought back a laugh, and feeling suddenly playful, she abruptly switched subjects. "Martin? You really are for Donnelly, aren't you? Now that we're going to be married, you can tell—"

He growled, and before she realized what had happened, he had pulled her over into his lap. Nipping at her lips, he said laughingly, "That, you crazy, wonderful clown, is exactly what I mean. I want you to spend the rest of your life taking me by surprise."

She ran adoring fingers through his hair and then down along his lean cheek. "I can do that." Tilting her head sideways, her hazel eyes twinkling up at him, she added, "I can make custard, too. Let's keep that in mind when we're picking out wallpaper for the master bath."

His rich laughter filled the small interior of the car. Satisfied with his reaction, Cara wound her arms around his neck, her eyes devouring his tempting lips. As she watched, she read her name in them as he silently, almost reverently told her of his love, before covering her mouth with his. The scorching kiss took her breath, and any desire to speak, away.

The Silhouette Cameo Tote Bag Now available for just $6.99

Handsomely designed in blue and bright pink, its stylish good looks make the Cameo Tote Bag an attractive acces- sory. The Cameo Tote Bag is big and roomy (13″ square), with reinforced handles and a snap-shut top. You can buy the Cameo Tote Bag for $6.99, plus $1.50 for post- age and handling.

Send your name and address with check or money order for $6.99 (plus $1.50 postage and handling), a total of $8.49 to:

**Silhouette Books
120 Brighton Road
P.O. Box 5084
Clifton, NJ 07015-5084
ATTN: Tote Bag**

SIL-T-1R

The Silhouette Cameo Tote Bag can be pur- chased pre-paid only. No charges will be accep- ted. Please allow 4 to 6 weeks for delivery.

N.Y. State Residents Please Add Sales Tax

Offer not available in Canada.

AMERICAN TRIBUTE

Where a man's dreams count for more than his parentage...

Look for these upcoming titles under the Special Edition American Tribute banner.

CHEROKEE FIRE
Gena Dalton #307—May 1986
It was Sabrina Dante's silver spoon that
Cherokee cowboy Jarod Redfeather couldn't
trust. The two lovers came from opposite
worlds, but Jarod's Indian heritage taught
them to overcome their differences.

NOBODY'S FOOL
Renee Roszel #313—June 1986
Everyone bet that Martin Dante and Cara
Torrence would get together. But Martin
wasn't putting any money down, and Cara
was out to prove that she was nobody's fool.

MISTY MORNINGS, MAGIC NIGHTS
Ada Steward #319—July 1986
The last thing Carole Stockton wanted was to
fall in love with another politician, especially
Donnelly Wakefield. But under a blanket of
secrecy, far from the campaign spotlights,
their love became a powerful force.

AM-TRIB-1R

AMERICAN TRIBUTE

American Tribute titles now available:

RIGHT BEHIND THE RAIN
Elaine Camp #301–April 1986
The difficulty of coping with her brother's
death brought reporter Raleigh Torrence
to the office of Evan Younger, a police
psychologist. He helped her to deal with
her feelings and emotions, including love.

THIS LONG WINTER PAST
Jeanne Stephens #295–March 1986
Detective Cody Wakefield checked out
Assistant District Attorney Liann McDowell,
but only in his leisure time. For it was the
danger of Cody's job that caused Liann to
shy away.

LOVE'S HAUNTING REFRAIN
Ada Steward #289–February 1986
For thirty years a deep dark secret kept them
apart–King Stockton made his millions while
his wife, Amelia, held everything together.
Now could they tell their secret, could they
admit their love?

Available July 1986

Silhouette Desire

Texas Gold

The first in a great new Desire trilogy by Joan Hohl.

In *Texas Gold* you can meet the Sharp family—twins Thackery and Zackery.

With Thackery, Barbara Holcomb, New York model, embarks on an adventure, as together they search for a cache of stolen gold. For Barbara and Thack, their gold is discovered in the bright, rich vein of their love.

Then get to know Zackery and his half sister Kit in *California Copper* and *Nevada Silver*—coming soon from Silhouette Books.

DT–1RA

One of America's best-selling romance authors writes
her most thrilling novel!

TWIST OF FATE

JAYNE ANN KRENTZ

**Hannah inherited the anthropological papers that could
bring her instant fame. But will she risk her life and give
up the man she loves to follow the family tradition?**

Available in June at your favorite retail outlet, or reserve your copy for
May shipping by sending your name, address, and zip or postal code
along with a check or money order for $4.70 (includes 75¢ for postage
and handling) payable to Worldwide Library Reader Service to:

In the U.S.
Worldwide Library
901 Fuhrmann Blvd.
Buffalo, NY
14269

In Canada
Worldwide Library
P.O. Box 2800, 5170 Yonge St.
Postal Station A, Willowdale, Ont.
M2N 6J3

BPA—TOF-H-1

 WORLDWIDE LIBRARY

COMING NEXT MONTH

MISTY MORNINGS, MAGIC NIGHTS—Ada Steward
Recovering from a recent divorce, Carole Stockton had no desire for another involvement. Then politician Donnelly Wakefield entered her life and he was determined to be a winning candidate.

SWEET PROMISE—Ginna Gray
At eighteen, Joanna fell in love with Sean Fleming. But he only considered her a spoiled child. Could she convince him of the promise of a woman's love?

SUMMER STORM—Patti Beckman
When political cartoonist Leida Adams's sailboat capsized, she couldn't tell her handsome lifesaver, Senator Grant Hunter, that he was the target of her biting satire. Would the truth keep their love from smooth sailing?

WHITE LACE AND PROMISES— Debbie Macomber
After high school, Maggie and Glenn drifted apart and suffered their private heartaches. Years later at their old friends' wedding, they fell in love. They were determined to bury their pasts and trust their rediscovered happiness.

SULLIVAN VS. SULLIVAN—Jillian Blake
Kerry and Tip were attorneys on opposite sides of a perilous case. The situation was getting hotter by the minute. They could agree to a compromise, but only if the verdict was love.

RAGGED RAINBOWS—Linda Lael Miller
Shay Kendall had grown up overshadowed by her actress mother's faded Hollywood fame. When exposé writer Mitch Prescott convinced her to collaborate on her mother's biography, she knew that he would free her from her haunting past and share her future.

AVAILABLE THIS MONTH:

NOBODY'S FOOL
Renee Roszel

THE SECURITY MAN
Dixie Browning

YESTERDAY'S LIES
Lisa Jackson

AFTER DARK
Elaine Camp

MAGIC SEASON
Anne Lacey

LESSONS LEARNED
Nora Roberts